The Pintlers

Majestic They Stand

by

Nola Ann Imus

and

Charlotte Wray McLucas

The Gilted Edge

Nola Imus and Charlotte McLucas
-Photo taken at Pintler Lake-

      The co-authors both reside at Newman Lake, Washington, some twenty miles from their birthplace, Coeur d'Alene, Idaho. With their families they have visited the very regions that pertain to this story. They have researched, documented and provided true accounts as to weather conditions and economic events. This writing is fiction based on fact, but written in a style to bring out the true emotions, temperament, and characteristics of their characters and how conditions affected and influenced these pioneers. Anecdotes and stories of the Pintlers settling the west have been passed down through the generations, and are an integral part of this book woven within it's pages.
      The authors each share a love of nature and a flair for creativity. They have previously researched and written a local history for a successful community fund-raiser, Recipes and Memoirs, that sold out after it's third printing. Both have equally shared in the research and writing of The Pintlers, Majestic They Stand.

In memory

of our father

William Augustus Pintler

1885-1976

*We are indebted to
Our mother, Florence Neelie Pintler
1897-1989*

*Our brother, Charles Newell
1919-1997*

*Our sister, Cleo Ione and our brother, Virgil Augustus
for their valuable contributions*

***

*Many thanks to our husbands
Paul and LeRoy
for their support and encouragement
throughout this writing*

Copyright 1997

Nola Ann Imus
and
Charlotte Wray McLucas

All rights reserved. No part of this book may be reproduced in any form, stored in a retrieval system or transmitted in any form or by any means, electronic, mechanical, photocopying, recording or otherwise without prior written permission of the publisher or authors.

Printed in the United States
First Printing

ISBN 0-9668372-0-7

The Gilted Edge
P.O. Box 484
Newman Lake, WA 99025

INTRODUCTION

The Anaconda Pintler Wilderness which lies in the Beaverhead, Bitterroot and Deerlodge National Forests in Montana State now stands in majestic tribute to Charles Ellsworth Pintler. He was a man who typified the very lifestyle of this designated area.

How appropriate in the course of events that when the Wilderness Act was passed on September 3, 1964, these words were included, 'A wilderness, in contrast with those areas where man and his own works dominate the landscape, is hereby recognized as an area where earth and it's community of life are untrammeled by man, where man himself is a visitor who does not remain', for Charles Ellsworth Pintler was also a visitor. He remained there for a mere three years. Towns around this wilderness still echo his presence. The mountain range is referred to simply as *The Pintlers*.

Mere words cannot do justice to the magnificent Anaconda Pintler Wilderness in southwestern Montana. The 159,068 acres of high, rugged and beautiful mountain scenery in the Bitterroot, Beaverhead and Deerlodge National Forests, challenges today's hiking and backpacker enthusiasts, mountain climbers, llama and horseback riders to experience the full impact of it's awesome majesty by setting foot in it's vast nature world.

Less than a two hour drive from Butte, Dillon or Hamilton, the wilderness spans about forty miles along the Continental Divide in Beaverhead, Deerlodge, Granite and Ravalli Counties.

Elevations range from 5400 feet at Willow Flats on the east fork of the Bitterroot to 10,783 feet at West Goat Peak. The alpine zone consists of talus rock slopes, small lakes, meadows and tundra-like plants similar to those in the arctic.

Craggy mountain peaks tower above a forested floor. Snowfields lie nearly dormant, melting, then freezing, sometimes the year round. Snowstorms can appear any time of the year, even in July and August.

Sparkling streams fed by snowbanks above timberlines, tumble down steep canyons from high mountain meadows. Mountain goats make their home on it's peaks, elk with their calves feed in mountain meadows, a variety of flora and fauna flourish. Glacial cirques and alpine lakes can be viewed, rainbow and cutthroat trout lure the fisherman to the lakes and streams.

Forty five miles of the Continental Divide National Scenic Trail lead through the Anaconda Pintler Wilderness, and is known to be some of the best scenery of the 3,100 mile trek that will eventually link Canada and Mexico.

Presently there are about two hundred eighty miles of Forest Service system trails within this wilderness.

A sense of the past surrounds the adventurer in these mountains. Looking south down toward the Big Hole Valley one can view an emerald vale twenty miles wide and stretching out for eighty miles into a crescent shaped basin.

This land is rich in history. It was on July 6, 1806 that the first white men, Lewis and Clark, on their famous expedition, saw the Big Hole Valley. They had their noon day lunch at the hot springs near Jackson. Clark said that this was one of the most beautiful valleys he had seen, called attention to the number of fur bearing animals in the streams, and the lush grasses that covered the plains.

The character of the land is still similar to what it was when they observed it. A hiker can feel the same natural beauty and accomplishment an early day explorer must have felt.

Natural ecosystems are now protected for future generations.

In today's world, camping gear is deemed essential, hiking trails and signs are laid out, published maps, hiking and guide books lead the adventurer over the wilderness trails.

When settling the west, no guide showed the early mountain men and trail blazers where to camp, where to find the next water hole, which firewood made clear coals and which would only smoke.

Mountains, peaks, creeks and lakes, the whole mountain range was nameless until after this region was home to pioneer and trail blazer, Charles Ellsworth Pintler in 1885.

Even today, he and these wide expanses of forested mountains help shape our youth. Hiking and backpacking are a popular recreation in today's stressful world. The Anaconda Pintler Wilderness is a place and purpose of untamed nature. It is a useful land resource, it exercises the body, stimulates the mind, and renews the soul in a search for solitude, just as it did to Charles Ellsworth Pintler over a century ago.

TABLE OF CONTENTS

HEADING WEST	1
BLUE MOUNTAIN HOMESTEAD	10
CHARLIE AND KATIE	18
SOUTH MOCCASIN BOUND	26
UNEXPECTED LAYOVER	31
OUT ON THE PRAIRIE	33
SETTLING IN THE BIG HOLE	37
GRIZZLY ATTACK	40
KATIE'S DILEMNA	45
TRIP TO ANACONDA	49
NUGGET ON A SHOESTRING	57
KATIE MEETS SEVEN DOG JOHNSON	64
THE BLIZZARD OF 1886-1887	69
BANNACK CITY AND HOME AGAIN	75
CHARLIE FACES A MAJOR CONFLICT	86
OFF TO JUDITH BASIN	89

JOYS AND TRAGEDIES	93
GILTEDGE AND THE DEPRESSION	98
LIFE ON BEAVER CREEK	107
BY RAIL TO OREGON	113
RETURN TO COEUR D'ALENE	119
JOURNEY'S END	125
EPILOGUE	130
A WINDOW TO THE REST OF THE STORY	136
BIBLIOGRAPHY AND RESOURCES	159

Chapter 1

HEADING WEST

Young Charles picked up his gun belt and buckled it around his slender waist. Excitement sounded in his voice when he told Ed for the third time he never thought he'd ever be in Council Bluffs, Iowa.

His eyes swept over the grounds to see men, women and children packing wagons to head out west. Some were hungry for land or a fresh start in life or in Charles' case, a thirst for the wilderness. He had dreamed of joining a wagon train ever since he could remember.

Charles, dressed in a flannel shirt, dark trousers with suspenders and a plaid mackinaw, mounted his pony and looked around for a last time at this temporary camp of the last two weeks.

Under his wide brimmed hat he saw cattle grazing on dew covered grass. Saddle ponies stepped and snorted impatiently in confined quarters in this unfamiliar setting. He smiled when he saw Ed, tall and lean, in buckskin jacket and jeans move with ease as he added one last item to the load. Charles rode over beside the wagon with his own wagon load of dreams, eager for departure, when he heard the wagon master's command to move 'em up, head 'em out.

Slowly the wagons began to roll.

Some rode saddle horses, but most trudged along on foot. A loose herd of milk cows plodded along behind the canvas covered wagons.

Charles rode tall and proud in the saddle. His dark hair blew in the wind. With his fair skin tender as the morning sun, he seemed almost too young to strike out on his own. His sincere eyes smiled at Ed, then he switched from a walk to a canter to survey the wagon train. The year----1870. The lad, Charles Ellsworth Pintler heading west.

Half a days ride later, Charles found himself deep in thought about his family he left behind in his birthplace of Winona, Minnesota. His thoughts rambled on of his brothers, Austin and Jud, and sisters Effie, Nellie and Molly. He remembered the talk that he and Ed had with his father, Augustus, and mother, Eliza, before they left home. They sat around the kitchen table in their farm home. Cups steamed as they sipped coffee and considered the possibilities of the travel west until they finally decided the opportunity seemed too good to pass up. The land of tall trees and deep valleys that brimmed with rich soil beckoned them. He and Ed would pave the way out west. Charles' family would follow later.

It was a memorable day when he left home with a strong shake of his father's hand and his mother's kiss and fervent Christian blessing in his ear.

He could still see his mother's tear filled eyes as she stood on the porch and watched them pull out. With misty eyes and a lump in his throat, he kicked his horse to move along. He wiped tears with one hand while he held the reins with the other.

They had outfitted themselves all winter for this trip. His dream was finally reality. His heart raced with anticipation as he rode on, absorbed the area and what lay ahead.

Days wore on, deep grasses swayed, changed color and now took on a gold tinge as the sun sank in the western sky. Days later brush and buffalo grass appeared and lay flattened for miles around from earlier buffalo herds. Sometimes Charles saw small herds of buffalo graze in the gullies. He watched these huge, magnificent animals in awe as he prodded his horse to move on.

Days wore into weeks. Weeks into a month.

The weathered wagon wheels caught Charles' eye only to remind him of the many laborious hours ahead over more sagebrush, rocks and mudholes. A great, cloudless sky, and nothing else but the rolling ocean of grass lay ahead. He settled into a monotonous pattern, letting his body roll along with the prairie.

Days later found them with no shelter from the sun. Wide brimmed hats and sunbonnets offered only a speck of shade. The men donned bandannas around their faces. People trudged through dust ankle deep. Dust took a toll on the cattle, horses and oxen. Days that followed were the same. Dust was everywhere. Sand sifted into the wagons. They had to stop for blowing dust.

The joyous, enthusiastic group of people who left full of spirit were now apprehensive. They grew short tempered and tongues were sharp for no apparent reason. Children burst into tears at the slightest provocation.

Again at days end, Charles watched the white sun turn to gold, then red and sink below the western horizon across the gloomy dust strewn prairie. He wiped his irritated eyes and looked down at his scuffed boots covered with dirt and grime. He had been real proud of these boots when he left home and realized that this journey was darn tough. He rubbed his hands together and felt sandy grit on his chapped skin.

That night, a violent roar of thunder shook the travelers from sleep. Cracks of lightning spread across the open sky. Huge drops of rain pelted the camp. Then it stopped only to come down harder than ever. Everything was soaked. It rained all the next day. Finally the downpour lulled and warm sunlight streamed across the prairie.

The wagons continued following the deep, worn ruts of the Oregon trail. It was more bearable to travel that morning even with miserable mud holes.

Charles rode along and watched the sun cast dark, variable shadows from the wagons' wheels as they edged through water covered mud holes over uneven ground. He noticed the wagons steamed as the sun's heat dissipated the water from their surface. The scent of wild sage and wet canvas surrounded him. His eyes caught shallow graves and deserted furniture that had been left by earlier travelers along this trail. Biting mosquitoes caused frustration and disgust. The monotonous scene stretched out ahead of him and for the first time he wondered where this would lead.

A welcome layover awaited them at the junction of the Laramie and North Platte Rivers. The screech of hubs rang loud as the wagons slowly circled and creaked to a stop. Streaked with grime, sweat with dirty clothes, the people were just thankful for the welcome reprieve. The children flitted about as lively as birds just released from a cage.

Some tents were set up for the night. Guards were posted as usual.

The bunch of weary travelers rested up that evening and retired early as they planned the morning's arrival of hard work.

The air felt fresh and clean on Charles' face as he brushed his horse's mane and tail. He looked up and noticed one man treating sores on his horses' neck where the collar had rubbed continuously. Others mended harnesses and worked on broken wagon wheels. Women washed loads of dirty laundry and hung them to dry.

Charles saw a few scouts ride in with freshly killed antelope and everyone settled down more at ease as that night they would get their bellies full.

Blue smoke rose and formed a haze over the grounds as the campfires simmered pots of beans. Hunks of roasting antelope hung above the fire. Women bustled about making vinegar pies for dessert.

After supper everyone spruced and duded up. Women decked out in freshly cleaned calico dresses. Some men with newly trimmed beards and mustaches had their hair slicked back with pomade of bear grease and lavender.

They all sat around campfires and wagons ready for an enjoyable evening. Lively card games took place, laughter followed an occasional joke. Some sat and enjoyed quiet conversations as mothers cuddled little ones in their arms.

With a pleased expression on his face, one fellow sauntered over to the wagon, took a fiddle from it's dusty case and struck out a catchy tune. Then squatted on heel, hat brim slouched to one side, he resined up his bow and entertained. Soon a harmonica joined in melody. People clapped hands to keep time with the rhythm. One couple danced about, others joined in. Another called for a square dance.

In the light of the campfire's flicker, Charles saw long skirts as they whirled to the music and someone called another round of the Virginia Reel. He looked on past the dancers to the far side of the wagon's circle. Men were gathered with cigarettes that dangled from their lips and a bottle of booze was passed generously.

Charles took in these happenings and wondered about the diversity of all these people. Two days before the same group was anxious and some felt hopeless, spirits were low.

Now, some whooped and hollered, and finally one by one, they turned in for the night. He found amusement just to sit, watch and learn.

The wagons rolled on again the next morning. They met weary but enthusiastic travelers headed eastwardly, back home from the west. Many times along the trail they came upon caravans headed the same direction so they traveled together. Sometimes the travelers parted and each headed their own way to forage for grass, fuel and water as these three elements were often scarce. Occasionally they met up later with the same people at another point on the trail.

They camped at Independence Rock like so many caravans of wagons did before them and marveled at the panoramas that lay ahead.

After the caravan was approached by friendly Indians, Charles rode along and his thoughts flashed back to when he was nine years old. Redskins came to mind. His thoughts were more vivid than ever. The Civil War was raging in it's third year. There were tomahawks, piercing arrows and blood. Bodies that had been scalped by redskins lay etched in his memory. Brutality was strong on both sides.

The family farm in Winona had held its own with his mother in charge. There was no choice. His father, a lieutenant, lay wounded in battle at Vicksburg. He had wondered if he would ever see his father again .

His shoulders grew heavy as he had second thoughts about this trip west.

He pushed himself hard, then remembered his father's pride when he returned home from the war. His father had learned of his heroic deeds while he was away. He remembered his father told him he knew he was no quitter. He smiled. His knew his dad was behind him all the way.

His thoughts turned to his mother. She was a good size smaller than most women. He remembered how she stood up against all odds when others had fled their homes during Sioux attacks.

Once again strength and courage flowed through his veins. He settled back in the saddle and let the western prairie draw him forward. He knew then he would reach that wilderness.

They crossed over a broad rolling prairie covered with sage, then between two mounds called South Pass. Tree covered mountains showed to the northwest, their peaks covered with snow. They headed down the other side and made camp. There was good grass and ponds of water.

Charles felt renewed as they left camp the next day. Wild sage dotted the area on the next day's travel. Further on into their travels were aspen trees. Later appeared pine and spruce groves and then their travels led them onto valleys, rivers, streams and more hills. The beautiful scenery confirmed his belief he had made the right decision when he followed his heart.

They forged many streams and followed the river. Their pathway was on the rim of a steep hill with treacherous trails. Below the rushing water snaked it's way through a deep canyon to meadows with grassy areas. Onward they continued to follow the river and arrived at The Dalles and then Cascades. Then they took a ferry across the Columbia.

Mt. Hood loomed in the distance and snow capped mountain peaks showed to the north as they headed toward Oregon City. The caravan arrived there nearly six months after their journey began.

The great scheme that had driven Charles to the heart of the frontier suddenly came to a dismal halt. He found the land of milk and honey he had dreamed of was not the peaceful unsettled wilderness he had envisioned, but instead Oregon City bustled with activity and earlier settlers. Beset by loneliness and doubt he stuck out the mild, rainy, but lonely winter.

Optimism filled his heart when he received a letter from his father. His parents were headed out west come spring.

Patent

United States

The United States of America

To all to whom these presents shall come, Greeting:

Certificate No. 561. Whereas Augustus T. Pindlis of Columbia County, Washington Territory, has deposited in the General Land Office of the United States a certificate of the Register of the Land Office at Walla Walla, Washington Territory, whereby it appears that full payment has been made by the said Augustus T. Pindlis according to the provisions of the Act of Congress of the 24th of April 1820 entitled "An Act making further provision for the sale of the Public lands" and the Acts supplemental thereto, for the North East quarter of the South West quarter, the South half of the North West quarter, and the North West quarter of the South West quarter of...

Homestead filed in 1878, Dayton, Columbia County, Washington Territory

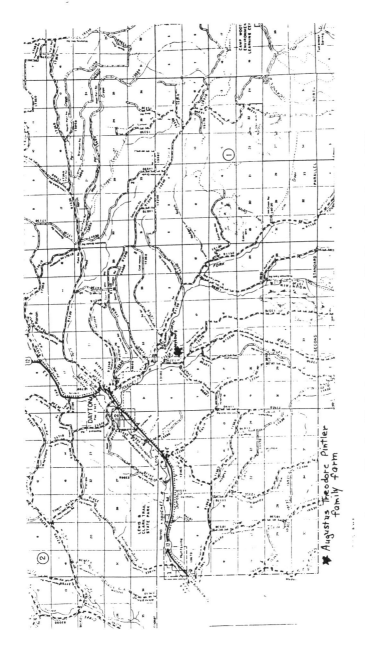

Augustus Theodore Pintler homestead in Dayton, Washington Territory in 1878

Charles and Ed worked for other settlers and earned their room and board as they cleared and fenced land, cut hay and made fence posts.

Months later, another letter reached Charles. Their journey west had been delayed and a sister, Winnie had been born. The westward caravan had to stop in Wyoming Territory and spend the winter in the Rocky Mountains. His folks would arrive the following spring and planned to head toward Columbia County, probably the town of Dayton.

Charles and Ed worked their way around the rugged Cascade Mountain range, and settled in Dayton awaiting their family.

In 1874 their family arrived and settled in Columbia County, Territory of Washington. They homesteaded southeast of Dayton along the Touchet River about one and a half miles outside of town.

Charles grew more restless each day, but he and Ed worked to help their father for the next few years. He consoled himself knowing he couldn't file on a homestead until he was twenty one years old. He knew he had to stick it out here, but he still dreamed of living in the wilderness.

Chapter 2

BLUE MOUNTAIN HOMESTEAD

Early in 1878, Charles headed out to re-check some property. He had visited the place the fall before and liked it. If it wasn't already filed on, he would homestead there.

Charles donned his new brimmed hat and buckskin jacket and swung into the saddle. He rode his black gelding due north from Dayton and on through rolling hills.

As he looked ahead, grass widows gave the meadows a purple hew. Ducks had appeared along the river bank, and he knew that spring had arrived. He followed the river's southern flank and continued on through tall fields of grass.

Charles liked this country, but it wasn't his kind of country. He reached Jawbone Flats on the eve of the second day. He followed the old-Nezperce Trail and crossed the river at Red Wold Crossing. He spent the night camped on the other side. Early in the morning he continued south for a spell and then in a southeasterly direction toward the mountains. Barren country followed except scatterings of sage. Cottonwood trees grew along creek banks. As he headed further south into higher elevations, he noticed several creeks flowed downward in a northerly direction.

The mountains hung in the misty distance, shadowy, changing and elusive. Charles knew if he hadn't visited the area before he would not have known if it were mountains or a mirage. Further on, there were now birch and occasional pine. Higher elevations showed cedar, fir and open conifer forests.

He camped that nightfall on a nameless creek in the northern edge of the timbered area of the Blue Mountains. There was prime pasture, good water, and timber. He would have plenty of room for livestock and the mountains were full of game.

He staked the boundaries of the 160 acre parcel. Then he rode north and filed his homestead rights, headed back home and made it back on the fourth day.

Excitement showed in his voice as he relayed the information to Ed that he had filed the claim about three miles north of Anatone. He told Ed that the adjoining 160 acres was clear. Ed filed on the property that joined Charles.

The sound of axes rang out as the two young men cleared the land and built pole fences around their holdings. Shavings flew as they drew the crosscut saw forward and back to cut logs. They hauled logs from the nearby mountains and built their cabins on a nameless creek, Charles on the south and Ed's on the north. The land was abundant with rocks. Charles added a rock fireplace to his cabin.

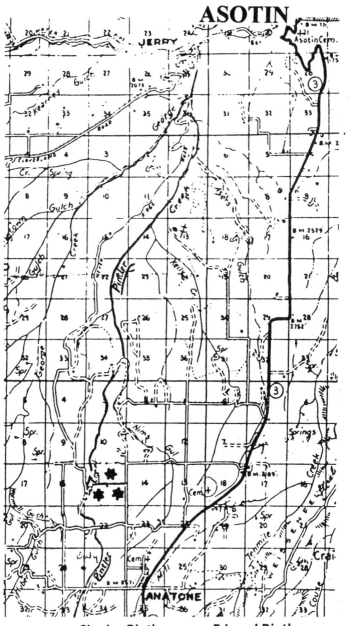

★ Charles Pintler ★ ★ Edward Pintler

Map of that part of Asotin County showing Pintler Creek

They bought livestock and settled down in the wilderness.

Ed worked and took care of the livestock on his homestead. He was contented as his wife, Mary was now at his side.

Charles tended his livestock, but every chance he had he would head to the mountains to hunt, trap and gather furs to sell. He felt excitement as he hiked these mountains, as each hour of the day it showed different mysteries that it held. As he trekked the Blue Mountains he found varied colored basalt that topped some of the high peaks. In other areas alpine lakes held melted snow that seeped and spilled down the mountainside to form streams. He stood and looked far below at a roaring river that channeled it's way through a deep canyon of 6,000 feet. He felt humbled as he walked through majestic forests as the sun cast misty shadows on the mossy ground. The damp, earthy smell and the quietude surrounded him as he sat beside a stream and his spirits were filled.

By late fall he had collected a small supply of pelts, so with renewed hope he continued trapping through winter.

He hand-made snowshoes of willows. He bent and dried these into shape and then laced them with leather strips. He could walk much easier now, even in the deepest snow.

Winter brought deep snow pack. Sudden storms ravaged the mountains in the higher elevations.

Some nights Charles spent on the mountain. He would choose an overhang on the edge of a rock cliff, build a fire on the edge and sleep between the fire and the cliff. The wind howled and snow blew, but the place he chose added protection and warmth. He always slept on his stomach as he didn't catch a cold easily that way.

Charles made numerous trips to the mountains that winter and soon it was springtime. He stepped outside his cabin door and breathed the fresh mountain air deep into his lungs. He looked around at his and Ed's accomplishments of the last two years and a half smile crossed his face. Spirits lifted, he decided to visit the new family that moved in 'bout a mile over.

As he saddled his pony, Ed stood and leaned against the edge of the doorway of his cabin and watched his younger brother. He noticed the changes in him since they came out west and figured he'd grown into quite a man. The complexity of Charles puzzled Ed though, on one hand he liked secluded wilderness and on the other he enjoyed a visit with about every greenhorn or experienced westerner that he ran in to. It was easy for Charles to make friends and he seemed to know most everyone from Alpowa City Way Station by the Snake River to the top of the Blue Mountain range, and everyone in between.

Old building in Anatone, Washington
(Photo taken recently)

Charles mounted his gelding, waved and was off. Ed smiled and waved back. He rode the mile to the new settler's cabin. When he neared the barn, he saw a man who was giant in physique feeding some livestock. He introduced himself to the stranger. The man stopped his work and leaned on his pitchfork. After a long conversation, Charles learned that William Ira Dundom and wife Kate, had immigrated from Holland. This Dutchman was over six feet tall, and weighed upwards of two hundred fifty pounds. He spoke in a guttural voice of heavy Dutch accent.

Charles learned the Dundom family had left Rotterdam, Holland, when daughter Katie was a year old, only a babe in a wooden cradle. Charles noticed his face was lined with self-confidence as he stood telling his story. He relayed to Charles about the voyage across the sea and the settlement in Pennsylvania. They moved on to St. Louis, Missouri and he told of his work building the railroad. He found it an extremely unsanitary place to live so his family gathered their goods and headed west.

Charles inquired what part of the west they had settled.

William said they had ended up in Montana Territory where the youngest daughter, Mary was born near Gallatin City three years before.

Charles leaned forward and crossed his hands on the saddlehorn as he listened and inquired what had brought them here.

Charles saw the anguish in his face as he told of two neighbor women being scalped by Indians. He said it was then they headed for Washington Territory. There was another Indian outbreak after they arrived, so his family was forced to live in an Army stockade for a few months. Then they made their way to the Alpowa Way Station and settled in this area.

Charles noticed he stood with his fingers curled in suspenders that were fastened to a heavy pair of twill pants. His red and black plaid flannel shirt brought Charles attention to the red socks inside his size 13 shoe. He watched as William lifted a sizable hand to smooth his trim mustache and beard.

His wife, Kate stepped outside the cabin door with a wash basin in her hands. A small, wiry lady and full of energy, Charles guessed her to be about five feet tall and maybe a hundred pounds. She threw the water from the basin and whirled back inside. With a flash of his eyes and a nod, Charles shook William's hand and headed back to his homestead to help his brother fix fence.
William invited him to stop by anytime.
The next week on his way to check traps, he decided he'd stop by Dundoms. It was a windy but sunny day as he rode up on his buckskin pony. As he approached the side of the cabin, he spotted someone hanging up clothes. A young lady had just pinned a pair of overalls to the line as he rode up. Dust flew from his pony's hooves. Katie, the young lady, looked up sharply, her dark eyes snapped. She told him he could be more considerate.
Charles liked the looks of this little Dutch girl, but she sure had spunk. Later, whatever task he would work on throughout the day, he found his thoughts on the little Dutch lady by the name of Katie. He would chance by the Dundoms, talk about the weather, the land he had just fenced, or a settler who had just filed a claim. He did anything to pass the time of day and get on the good side of Katie's father. He didn't spot Katie, but his thoughts were still on her. On his next trip to Dundoms he apologized to Katie and she accepted his apology.
Charles smiled, waved and rode off. Katie managed a weak smile and wave from the porch for fear her mother or sister might have been watching. Katie looked forward to meeting Charles again.
Her father didn't know, but Katie did take long summer walks and secretly meet Charles. She learned of his tender heart, hardy soul, and adventurous nature. She grew to admire him and wondered if she could really be in love. She began saying Charlie, Charles just sounded too formal for her. She remembered how he looked at her the first time she said Charlie, she could tell he was

pleased. She pulled the covers up around her shoulders that night in bed and giggled to herself about her thoughts of Charlie.

Charles became more fond of Katie and told her father so. William told Charles he was too bold and experienced for his young innocent daughter.

Chapter 3

CHARLIE AND KATIE

As if touched by an artist's brush the cottonwoods were covered with frost in a riot of colors that ranged from gold to crimson on either side of the wagon road. The road led to Lewiston, Territory of Idaho.

Sixteen year old Katie occasionally glanced at Charlie as he drove the team. Under his wide brimmed hat, she saw thick hair show dark against his fair skin. She never saw Charlie in a suit before, and in his new dark gray suit, he looked more handsome than ever to her. He was twenty-six, his sincere face unlined with unworried youthfulness.

Katie Cecelia Dundom sat proud and stately as she rode along side Charlie on the buckboard. A bonnet covered her dark complexioned skin and small face. Her hands lay folded in the lap of her long, full gathered skirt, which flowed down to cover her high button shoes. A fringed shawl completed her attire.

With twinkling eyes, Charlie occasionally spoke to Katie followed by his familiar wink. With a cupped hand, Katie covered her mouth and reacted with a little giggle. That amused Charlie, he could only guess what it meant.

They reached the Snake River and crossed by way of the Pearcy Ferry to reach Lewiston. They were married by Justice of the Peace, J.K. Vincent, November 10, 1880. They celebrated their vows, dined at the Madison Boarding House, and rented a room for one night.

There was a definite chill in the air on their return to the cabin on the creek. The team of horses jingled the rings on their harness bridles, as if to celebrate the event that had just taken place.

> Territory of Idaho
> Nez Perce County
>
> This Certifies that Charlie Pintler of Columbia Co. in the Territory of Washington and Katie C. Dunham of Columbia Co. in the Territory of Washington were at Lewiston in the said County by joined together in Holy Matrimony on the 10th day of November in the year of our Lord one thousand Eight Hundred and Eighty
>
> In Presence of
> Sel. D. Martin
> O. Monteith
>
> O. H. Vincent
> Justice of the Peace

They pulled up alongside the cabin. Charlie jumped down, walked around the wagon and put his arms up to lift Katie down. He carried her over the threshold into the cabin and sat her by the fireplace.

Katie's heart gave a funny little lurch as he smiled and looked directly into her eyes.

He lit the match to the kindling and topped it with dry pine logs. Flames licked it's crusty bark. The firelight showed his dark hair, broad brow and high cheekbones.

Instinctively, Katie arose and moved closer to him. It was as though she was seeking the warmth and comfort of his body.

Charlie turned, took his suit jacket off and then he took her in his arms.

In the morning Charlie picked up the water bucket, went to the creek and dipped a fresh bucket of water. Soon the teakettle steamed on the back of the cookstove.

Katie had helped her mother cook and was not unskilled when she took on the role of housewife. Her face smudged with flour, she rolled biscuits on the makeshift kitchen cabinet Charlie had built. She baked bread in the oven. She learned which wood made a quick fire and which baked the best bread.

Katie's homemade candles sat on tiny shelves on the wall on each side of the cookstove. Charlie had carved these ornate shelves by hand. The applebox cupboard held their staples.

Charlie's trusty rifle always hung above the door. Venison usually hung in the makeshift shed outside the cabin.

The mild winter passed. The country treated them to a glorious spring. Horse drawn plows opened the earth for the seed and the gentle rain.

The cabin's white, flour sack curtains Katie made dressed the windows. She looked out the window and saw morning glories as they wound their way toward the top of the cabin. She walked outside. The color and fragrance of wild rosebushes, service berries and gooseberries graced the outdoors.

Prairie chickens were abundant. Katie saved their soft feathers for her new quilt.

After supper Charlie strolled down the path to the creek's edge and dipped a bucket of water. A finch whistled from a tree branch across the creek, a cow bawled from a long way off. The spring's sweet scent of the evening mountain air drifted past him on

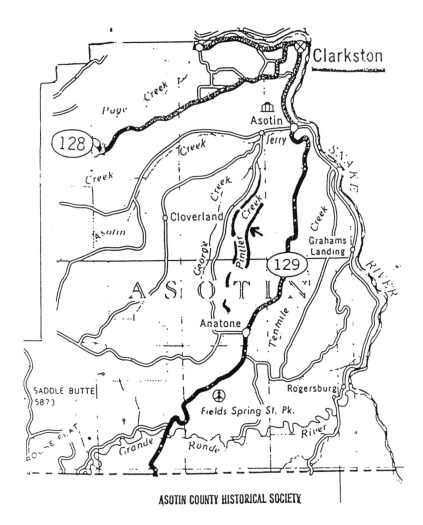

ASOTIN COUNTY

his way back to the cabin. He passed the stack of firewood piled high against the cabin.

Contentment filled his heart as he stepped inside and closed the cabin door.

Katie looked up from the dishpan and saw Charlie set the bucket on the table and hang his hat on a nail.

Later, he took his worn deck of cards from the shelf and sat at the kitchen table. By the light of the kerosene lamp he shuffled the cards several times and spread them evenly on the rough table top for a game of solitaire.

She gathered her quilt blocks and sewing basket and sat in the lamp's light and sorted through the fabric. Her fingers guided the needle stitch by stitch through the fabric and she wished for one of her mother's thimbles.

Charlie headed for the mountains as usual every chance he had. She often thought when he was away of the secret country walks she used to take to meet him. Going back in time, she remembered so well the twin trees along the trail and when they stood beneath their branches' shade and shared thoughts. She remembered this was where he asked for her hand in marriage, and she was so frightened to tell her folks. She could just smell the summer roses and most of all see the berry patch where she stopped to pick wild raspberries to take home to her mother. And, oh, the day she hoped he wouldn't notice the berry stain on her bodice collar when she met him.

The next time after Charlie left to trap, she picked up her lard pail and strolled on the country path. She came upon lots of berries, but few were ripe. Her slender fingers searched out ripe berries and dropped them in her pail. She reached for a couple nice plump ones, but when she arose she felt faint.

With the little pail of berries in hand, she with care, returned to the cabin.

By autumn, she was sure they would expect their first-born the following year.

Census of Asotin County, April 21, 1882
(Note signatures on lines 13, 14 and 15)

A T Pintler, brand placed on left shoulder.

Chas E Pintler, horses and cattle on left shoulder.

E A Pintler, cattle on left side.

Cattle brands of Augustus Theodore Pintler
Charles Ellsworth Pintler and Ed A. Pintler

Charlie decided to stay home, forget trapping and trekking in the mountains for a while when he learned of the expected new arrival. He had plenty of stock to attend and some small projects to do. He used a draw knife to peel small poles of pine to build a baby cradle. He fastened them together with pride.

Katie studied the creation and then studied Charlie and marveled at his creative hands.

That winter she and her mother sewed baby blankets and diapers, her mother knit baby clothes. In February of 1882 a baby girl was born. They named their pride and joy, Marguerite, but nicknamed her 'Nettie'.

Charlie knew he had even more reason to hunt for game and trap for he now had another mouth to feed. By this time, more experienced and with a larger trapping area, he gathered more furs to sell come spring.

Game was abundantly found here, although up higher only an experienced man could survive long in these mountains.

Charlie occasionally spotted other trappers in the area, but there were a few roughnecks, as some called them. There were some hiding out from the law and Charlie was concerned for Katie's and Nettie's safety. He began to teach Katie how to shoot the rifle for protection. By the end of the next few weeks Katie could shoot as good as any man. She felt more secure now when Charlie was gone.

Charlie and Katie visited Katie's folks often. William and Charlie talked at length each visit. He learned that Katie's father had a sense of humor, and he shook his head in dis-belief at another one of his stories. At that, William's face broadened, his cheeks flushed and he threw his head back as he broke into hearty laughter.

During one of their more serious conversations, William tried to convince Charlie they should start a horse ranch in the lush green meadows in central Montana Territory. He had heard where they could get four hundred head of Indian ponies by transferring their property. This offer enticed Charlie and he thought it could be a challenge. He looked up to this man and counted on him as being very knowledgeable. He mulled it over and over in his mind.

The next day Katie made a list of grocery items and Charlie headed for the town of Alpowa City. He would pick up supplies and the mail at the post office.

When he picked up the mail, the post master told Charlie he heard that a trapper had been killed. The man stated that some men went to check on him when they hadn't seen him for awhile, found his cabin door ajar. He was lying on his bed and when they walked over to check on him, found his head split wide open. Covered with blood. When they went to move him, his head rolled off. He had just sold his winter catch of furs and they stole the five hundred dollars he got paid for them.

Charlie was shaken. He knew it could have been him or his family as well. He had just sold a load of furs to the Hudson Bay Company Representative himself.

He hurried home to Katie and baby, concerned for their safety. He shuddered and tried to cast off the gruesome story he had heard.

He decided to take William up on his offer.

Katie couldn't understand why Charlie had a change of heart. She knew he loved this place and she did too. She didn't feel like traveling in a covered wagon. She glanced out the window and saw Charlie walk toward the creek. He looked up and saw Katie, smiled and winked, in his familiar way.

Charlie felt torn. He walked toward a hollow where a cluster of willows lay over the creek. His horses loved to drink from this spot and he loved it no less. He thought how many times in the middle of a hot summer day he had come down here to drink the fresh cold water. He felt an ache of sadness, a sense of loss at the thought of leaving. He wondered if he had made his mind up to leave for the right reason, or just for the adventure of the trip. But, he had also felt himself getting itchy feet again. He also felt a need to visit his mother and father before he left.

Katie stayed with her folks and Charlie headed for Dayton. He rode through hilly farming country. Along the Touchet River, surrounded by rolling hills he arrived at the A. T. Pintler family farm in Baileysbury, one and a half miles southeast of Dayton. His mother was in the kitchen, his dad was fixing fence.

Charlie always knew his mother to be a Christian woman, a counselor to the family, and he talked to her about leaving for Montana Territory. Whatever he chose to do, she advised him. He always knew he had her blessing.

He walked into the living room, the aroma of hot bread drifted from the oven in the kitchen. He gazed with an appraising eye at the family organ. He remembered the one he had seen abandoned on his travels out west on the Oregon Trail. He wondered how they ever managed to get this one over the Oregon Trail. He sat down at the organ. He sang with gusto and played his mother's favorite hymns. As she took bread from the oven she hummed along and the warm spiritual atmosphere floated off the living room walls. His heart felt light, he always felt a security and peace of mind in his family's home.

His dad stepped inside and offered a handshake. His grip was warm and strong. Charlie told him of the conflict he faced. He listened as his father told him he couldn't help him with the conflict but to weigh the consequences thoroughly before making any changes. He said he knew he would choose the right path, and he gave Charlie his blessing.

Chapter 4

SOUTH MOCCASIN BOUND

Charlie and William traded their homesteads for 400 head of Indian ponies. Early in 1885 the party lined up with supplies.

Charlie and Katie had bid Ed and Mary goodbye, as they had moved on to Garfield County where they had purchased some property.

Katie packed dishes, pots and pans and then baby clothes. Her eyes softened as she folded the baby quilt she had made and carefully tucked it along side her quilt in a lavender scented box.

Five other wagons joined the family for the journey. Charlie, William and his two sons, Willie and Ira, kept herd on the ponies and livestock. Daughters Fanny and Mary Dundom rode along side-saddle. Katie and her mother began their journey in the wagon, at times they trudged along side the wagon train. The caravan of wagons, ponies and livestock at last began their slow, difficult climb up the wagon road and lumbered across switchbacks.

They made their way to the top of the Lewiston hill half a day later. Ahead the rolling hills of the Palouse country came into view. Bands of horses and range cattle roamed over the prairie. Wild bunch grass stood high, the prairie wind blew night and day. After seven days travel, the herd of Indian ponies, wagon train and all forded Hangman Creek. They crossed over hilly regions, bypassed Fort Spokane and turned eastwardly and followed the Spokane River. The river wound it's way on toward the Pacific Ocean through a wide, flat expanse of land in this area. Bunch grass, nurtured by the moisture of melting mountain snow and spring rains, swished against the rider's stirrups The Indian ponies stopped to graze and had to be prodded along. On either side of this valley were hills with pine, fir, spruce and cedar trees. To the north were snow capped mountain peaks. Similar hills lay to the south and ahead to the east where their journey would take them.

Lofty, tree covered mountains could be seen in the distance.

They made camp on the Spokane River. A night chill rolled down from the hills. Over the peaks rose a full moon.

The next morning Charlie pushed his covers off, and rolled out from under the wagon. He walked down to the river and splashed his face with water. Boulders edged the river bank, sunflowers and small white daisies dotted the landscape. The beautiful scent of wild flowering syringa bushes drifted across the prairie. The lonesome cry of a mourning dove was heard.

After they ate, Charlie squatted, a tin cup of strong coffee in his hands and drank in the smoke of the fire. He wondered just where the evening camp fire would find them. It wouldn't be long before they forged the river, it's crossover was just a few miles ahead. He took in the peaceful setting but the mountains ahead mystified him. As he tended his horses, he shot a glance at the wagon to see the women tuck in the last of the breakfast dishes and cast iron skillets.

The caravan lined up and riders mounted their horses. Again the wagons rolled ahead. They made their way along the south side of the river. Here, they came upon the dried, bleached bones of hundred of ponies.

William reined up next to Charlie and conveyed that an Army Colonel, by the name of Wright and his troops captured the ponies from the Indians and shot them one by one. The shooting lasted for days. By the time they were done, close to six hundred were killed.

Near Spokane Bridge, William pointed out the best point to cross. The men went first and checked it out. They drove the cattle and Indian ponies across first. He and Charlie headed back across the river to help the wagons cross. Katie, now over seven months with child, clung to daughter Nettie and braced herself for the crossing. It went surprisingly well, soon the caravan of travelers was on the north side of the river. The caravan continued on following a deep rutted wagon road that led them over rocks, chuck holes, roots and snags toward Ft. Coeur d'Alene, Territory of Idaho.

Katie looked ahead as the sun danced across miles of crystal clear water. There was something about this lake, she had never seen one so beautiful in the wilderness and so big. Her eyes gazed at the mountains and green forests around it's banks. She hated to leave this peaceful setting, but the wagons jolted on following the lakeshore for miles.

The Mullan Trail took them over the Fourth of July Pass. A landmark, a mission built by Father Ravalli and the Coeur d'Alene Indians beckoned them.

The Sacred Heart Mission at Cataldo, Territory of Idaho. Built by Jesuist missionaries in 1853

The wagons slowed to a halt at the Cataldo Mission. Meal time was long past and food was in short supply, so they rationed what they had. Kate searched out some beef jerky and spread butter melted from the day's heat over thick slices of bread. They sat around the wagons and under the shade of trees and savored what they had.

The mission so intrigued Charlie, he cut his meal short to study the construction of the mission. Only then did he realize what could be accomplished with just a few tools. Not one nail was used in the building, just wooden pegs. He studied the upright timbers spanning twenty feet in length and dreamed of his own building in the wilderness.

They crossed over the Bitterroot Range, a more time consuming trek than they believed. Stomachs ached with hunger, Mary was sick, Nettie cried and tempers became short. Kate's dark eyes snapped. She glanced up at her husband's massive frame to the determined expression in his eyes, and wondered why he ever got the notion to go back to Montana Territory again. She remembered why they left a few years back, of the neighbor women who were scalped by Indians. The trip had taken it's toll.

Finally they reached Fort Missoula, an Army post built to watch over the settlers and control the Indians. The soldiers supplied them with an evening meal of beans. As they scarfed down their meal, Mary told her mother those beans were the best beans she ever ate.

William and Charlie replenished food and supplies which had drastically dwindled. They filled the wooden barrels with food and staples once again.

The wagon train followed the Bitterroot River through open country. Plains stretched out before them through the valley. To the west the valley followed the gigantic sierra of the breath-taking Bitterroot Mountain Range.

Charlie glanced toward the river, and his mind wandered. He'd like to try his hand at mining. Small discoveries of gold and silver sprung up right along. He continued forward and dreamed about gold panning, but knew they had to move ahead.

It had reached the hot month of July, time was near for the birth of Katie and Charlie's second baby. The sun beat down. Katie took her hanky from her skirt pocket and rubbed her tired eyes. She moistened her chapped lips. She knew not to complain, the worst was yet to come, she had learned to carry her burden, yet retain her charm.

They passed the IOU-IOU fork and the journey followed the valley's river to Nez Perce Creek, then turned northeast. The rutted wagon trail led them over prairie land toward the site of the Battle of Big Hole and they rolled to a stop. Sagebrush grounds echoed a sense of great loss. The caravan of travelers recalled the tragic event. The peaceful mountainous valley had become the site of a tragic and sad war. William relayed that it was eight years earlier Chief Joseph and his Nez Perce tribe were asleep when Colonel Gibbons troop fired down on them at dawn. Men, women and children were killed.

Charlie stood at a national monument erected on a grassy knoll. His rough fingers smoothed it's granite surface, his eyes lowered to read the inscription. Katie climbed down from the wagon. She reached her arm through the curve of his. As she studied the monument tears welled up in her eyes at the thought of the poor Indian women and children who were killed.

Charlie took a long deep look down into her troubled eyes. He hadn't really looked at her for awhile, and thought what a tough little woman she was and what he had put her through.

She raised a slender hand and brushed back dusty strands of hair from her face. She looked so young, despite her discomfort, worry and fatigue. He took her hand in both of his and assured her it wouldn't be much longer, they'd be in the South Moccasin Mountains.

Chapter 5

UNEXPECTED LAYOVER

On July 14, the travelers slept out under an overcast sky. It was a sultry night. Katie lay awake even more disturbed and restless than ever. Thoughts churned through her mind. The cows bellowed, a coyote howled from a long way off. That granite monument crept into her mind. The very grounds they were sleeping on haunted her, the mosquitoes didn't help.

Charlie said it wouldn't be long now to the South Moccasins, but oh, that seemed so far away to Katie. It was difficult to walk, and the jolting wagon was even worse.

Next morning they cooked over an open fire as Katie and her mother heard the men talk about the departure from the campsite. She was uncomfortable with the atmosphere but reluctant to start a day's travel. Agonizing pains gripped Katie, then others followed. She remembered when Nettie was born. This had gone on for several days before the birth. She dismissed the idea to not start on the next leg of the journey. Besides, the men were so trail happy, she just wouldn't tell them.

A lonely, deserted feeling was left hanging over the battleground site, the trampled grass and gray ashes lay here and there, for the wagon train had once again moved on surrounding the travelers with a strong scent of sagebrush and pine.

The creak and groan of the wagons echoed across the sagebrush flats.

The jolting wagon tossed Katie to and fro as it veered around boulders and chuck holes through the native prairie land. Katie heard the cows bawl, horse hooves clop and men talk of the horse ranch. She gritted her teeth. The creak of the wagon wore on her. She bit her lip and tried to hide the pain. Finally with stricken eyes she shouted at Charlie to halt the caravan.

He shot a glance at Katie. He shouted and motioned the caravan to stop, then slowed his team to rest apart from the others. He jumped down from the wagon seat, mounted Willie's saddled pony and sped to the Wisdom River two miles away.

William and Kate took charge inside the covered wagon, and tried to comfort their daughter till Charlie returned.

Men sat in the shade at the edge of wagons. Even though they knew the trip should not be delayed, they took pleasure in the reprieve. Some sat low on bent legs, spun yarns in low voices and others took a chew, wiped the sweat under hat bands and spoke of the last leg of the journey. The sun bathed mountain range to the north drew occasional glances. Women cooked over sagebrush fires that hot mid-summer day. Katie's sister, Mary engaged Nettie in games and stories. The entire caravan of pioneers went about as usual.

Charlie raced back on the sweating pony. Dust flew from the pony's hooves as he reined in and swung from the saddle. He dropped the reins and hastened inside with the precious water. Time seemed an eternity. Finally, came the cry of the newborn.

William delivered his grandson. His massive hands took the new-born and lay him on an Indian blanket Katie had cut into quarters. Kate tucked it around her new grandson. Charlie bent down and gazed at his little Dutch wife, holding the newborn in the curve of her arm, then moistened her lips with the valuable water.

The men talked long into the night. Charlie told William it was best Katie didn't travel yet, he and Katie would settle in the Big Hole, there was game in the mountains, plenty of creeks, rivers, and good summer pasture. William decided he and his family would continue on with the wagon train. He had to get those ponies on to central Montana Territory. Willie and Ira would help herd.

The next day Charlie located a spot for his family to settle by an everflowing creek close to the wagon road. The group eased their way over prairie land and stopped at the site. When William and Kate were assured of Katie's and baby's well being, they readied for departure.

Katie smiled through misty eyes and told her mother they had decided on the baby's name, William Augustus from both his grandfathers, but she would call him Billy. Her mother smiled and agreed what a grand name they had chosen, then insisted Katie needed her rocker.

William set the rocker on the ground beside the wagon, and Katie thanked them both. She knew her mother treasured this old rocking chair, she had it ever since she could remember.

This was the first time she would be apart from her family. The wagons moved out, dust rolled like clouds around the wagons and Katie watched them grow smaller and disappear in the distance. Tears filled her eyes. She wiped a tear with her apron and swallowed hard.

Charlie's attention turned to the rugged mountain peaks to the north, but he knew he had a load of work ahead of him before he could take off for the mountains.

They grew weary of the wagons but still had to live out of them until they set up a temporary living quarters.

Chapter 6

OUT ON THE PRAIRIE

It was a jeweled day of brilliant color, blue of sky and bright warm sunshine. Charlie picked up his ax and showed Katie where the cabin would be. He stepped off the dimensions. He drove a stake at each corner, pointed with his ax that the door would be facing west, due west. He said a worthy cabin should sit square with the earth itself. On his land he had the straightest virgin pine logs anywhere. The walls will be thick for the cold winter ahead.

Katie hung a kettle of pinto beans over the sage fire, and set a makeshift table along side the wagon. She heard the cows bawl, horses whinny, and the cry of her newborn, in the otherwise quiet prairie land.

That evening in a cluster of willows Charlie sat on a log and let his fish line down into a deep, dark hole in the rushing creek. Across the creek a distance away, a bull moose munched marshy grass. The mountain air brought a chill as he caught a string of skillet worthy trout. He headed back to the campsite, a willow pole in one hand and a string of trout in the other.

Katie wiped her brow with a wisp of her apron. The fresh trout curled in the cast iron skillet and turned a golden brown. She dipped the last batch in cornmeal, and they sizzled when she dropped them in the lard. They knew they could feed on them any time they took a notion.

Milk pail in hand, Charlie headed out to the wild pasture land. Wasn't long he lumbered back with a bucket of milk, with white foam two inches deep.

Katie put Nettie and baby William to bed, then snuggled in her bedroll. Her head lay on a soft feather pillow. She whispered a prayer for their safety, then for her family as they traveled on to the South Moccasins. She heard the coyotes howl and the creek chattering to the stars. She pulled the quilt up close, and it's scent of lavender stung her heart. She wondered what her mother would think if she could see the hard use this quilt was getting. They worked on it long evenings. Katie could just see her mother's tiny fingers guide the needle stitch by stitch around each block. She could smell the lavender fragrance her mother gave her to pack it in.

Charlie sat on a log by the fire late that night, poked a stick aimlessly as he hummed "Amazing Grace".

Katie watched him and thought he seemed so sure, so determined. He'd been looking at the mountains a lot lately, his thoughts were probably high in the mountains, his ears would even hear the padded step of a mountain lion. She snuggled deeper, started to giggle. She still thought he was handsome.

After a breakfast of cornmeal mush and fresh milk, Charlie saddled his horse and rode toward the Wisdom River. The calm river wound it's way in long, gentle curves through the basin. He followed it's northern bank over streams, bunchgrass and sagebrush, then crossed a new bridge. The wagon road led him to The Crossing. He sized up the town, then lit out for the General Store.

The man behind the counter glanced up. Charlie spoke and told him he was new in these parts. He rode over to see what the town had to offer. The bearded man acknowledged the handshake, took his black pipe from his mouth and wondered over from where.

Charlie told him they were camped over along the creek northeast for a spell. His name was Charlie Pintler. He had his family, his wife, little girl and a new baby boy who was born between waterholes, between the Wisdom River and the Big Hole Battlefield. Then they moved over to the creek.

The man replied that Charlie's son was one of the first white babies born in the Big Hole Basin. He said there weren't many settlers around here and wondered what the baby's name was. Charlie's lips curled in a grin when he told him his son's name was William Augustus, named after both his grandfathers. After that Charlie told the man his story. His dad was still in Washington Territory, Charlie settled there after he left Oregon City when he arrived out west. He didn't plan on this stay here, they were headed for central Montana Territory. He wondered if it'd work out best after all, he'd like to check out the mountains to the north. But for now, he'd settle over on the creek. He planned to put up a cabin and set foot on that mountain range.

The man replied that no one had explored much of that wild country yet.

Charlie told him he had an ax, but he could sure use that cross-cut saw stashed in the corner. He'd be cutting logs for the cabin. This little sidestep caught him by surprise.

Back at the campsite, Katie kept the campfire going, heated water in a black kettle that hung over the fire and scrubbed dirty clothes. She draped them here and there to dry. She saw a moose graze along the willows, antelopes came up to feed with the cows and saw a herd of elk feed near the hills. She hadn't shared words with anyone but Charlie since her family left for the South Moccasins. To her right she saw only the lonely wagon road. She glanced across the prairie, dusty, barren, so silent.

Looking north across the Big Hole Prairie
toward the mountain range known as *The Pintlers*

Suddenly her eyes caught sight of clouds of dust rolling up from the direction of the Wisdom River. She raised a hand above her brow and squinted against the wind to see a rush of ponies pound the earth as though they were coming straight for the campsite. She hastened to Nettie, then sped to Billy. She gathered them both, and stumbled close to the wagon. Chills raced up her spine. She thought the Indians may be racing their ponies again. If they weren't fishing along the river or hunting, they were either gambling or racing ponies. But she couldn't take any chances. She reached for her rifle, rested the barrel on the wagon.

Katie had never imagined in all her travels with a caravan how the rider's colors, their rich dark skin, and their ponies speed could alarm her so. The ponies gait finally slowed. She studied two of the Indians thirty feet from the wagon, others wandered or scattered across the basin. She stood not blinking and wondered what would become of this silent exchange, then darted her eyes from one stern faced rider to the other, and his half-smiling eyes. A gesture of his hand told her they were friendly so she lowered the rifle to her side. They remained silent, then Katie's shaky hands reached in the grub box, and offered them a half loaf of bread. At that, in a cloud of dust they whirled their ponies and raced off. Still trembly, she looked down at Billy and Nettie, felt a lump in her throat and put her forehead in her hands and fought the tears.

Chapter 7

SETTLING IN THE BIG HOLE

The morning had music of it's own, played out by the awakening wildlife, the squeak of leather, the clink of chains and the clop of horses' hooves.

Charlie directed his team of percherons as they pulled the wagon across the prairie. A couple miles later at the edge of timber, the sound of a cross-cut saw and ax echoed through the lodgepole pine forest. His rhythm never slowed and his eyes never wavered. He sawed to and fro till the tree's trunk tilted and plunged to the ground. His ax swung left, then right to limb. The handle of the ax slid to rest in his hand. He measured by ax lengths, notched then sawed twelve and fourteen foot logs. He picked up his kerosene in the corked bottle and poured some on his saw and leaned the bottle against a stump.

In the autumn sun-strewn days, sawdust and wood chips flew, pine scent perfumed the air. He brushed the chips from his shoulders and leaned on the ax handle to take a break. He wiped his sweaty forehead with his sleeve and took a swig of water.

Near sundown of another day the wagon creaked under a heavy load. His percherons pulled the load over the barest of the two-rutted trail through the unexplored wilderness and onto the prairie, back to Katie and the children.

A few weeks of back breaking work and he had enough logs to start his cabin. He swung his ax, hewed and shaped the log ends to fit together. At last the cabin was raised. A sod roof covered the earthen floored cabin. The outside of the cabin door he built of three twelve inch rough boards anchored in place by hinges of hammered steel. He had the steel hammered by a blacksmith over on the Noyes ranch.

Charlie walked over by the wagon and picked up an old bridle and salvaged a straight bit to make a door handle. He cut a slit through one end of a leather strap with his jack knife and spiked the strap to the door. The slit fastened over a hook.

A south window looked out over vast prairie land.

Charlie and Katie caulked the cracks with gumbo. The Montana mud dried hard as cement.

He built a loft in the east end of the cabin for their bed, and a small pole ladder to reach it. At the left of the door, he added some shelves. He cut logs ten inches in diameter into four foot sections, turned the round side down and fastened four half logs together for their table and added sturdy legs. He smoothed the top with a draw knife and made sturdy benches for each side of the table the same way.

He moved the cookstove inside.

Katie gathered sweet grass hay from the prairie, spread a soft surface and lay out her bedding. She covered it with her hand made quilt.

The tiny cabin was finished and the wilderness family moved in at last.

The Pintler cabin in the Big Hole Valley south of the Anaconda-Pintler Wilderness was built by Charles Ellsworth Pintler in 1885. It still stands today.
(Photo courtesy of US District Ranger, John Dolan)

Katie prepared the first meal since their move into the cabin by cutting and frying pieces of bacon in small bits, then removing the bacon and slicing potatoes in the grease. When they browned, she turned them over and added slices of onion on top, then the bacon bits. She seasoned this with salt and pepper. She added enough water to cover the potatoes so they would simmer slowly on the back of the wood stove. The satisfying aroma of the hot potatoes, onion and bacon filled the tiny cabin. Light bread biscuits completed the meal.

She mixed flour and potato water together and set it on the warming oven to make sourdough starter. She lit a piece of outing flannel soaked in grease and placed it in a can filled with tallow, it flickered from the homemade table by the window. This would have to do until the next trip to town, they would buy a lamp.

Cold air drifted across the prairie that night, so Charlie put another log in the fire, but his thoughts were once again on the mountain range to the north.

Chapter 8

GRIZZLY ATTACK

The sun shone brightly on the gray logs of the tiny cabin this early September morning. The air was clear and crisp as Charlie walked toward the shed to gather dried willow branches for a quick fire. Thick frost lay in the shade of the cabin. He glanced toward the mountain range to the north as he hurried back inside. Soon a fire blazed in the cookstove and when Katie awoke he told her he was headed out to scout, maybe bring back an elk for the meat this coming winter. He saddled his pony, packed some grub and headed north with the two pack horses.

She watched him disappear in the distance. She feared for his safety, then shrugged off the silly notion that something might happen to him. She turned and walked back to the cabin just glad that she had her rifle with her.

Charlie rode over sagebrush country and noted the sharp, brittle smell of the winter willows mingled with the sagebrush. He followed a rushing creek, then his trail led him to the edge of a pristine lake where he let his pony drink his fill. He noticed the winds had shifted the raft he had hewn that summer where he had it tied to a tree. He figured he wouldn't be using it to cross the lake again till next summer, if anything was left of it after winter, so he dismounted and pulled his raft up on the bank of dense underbrush.

Across the lake's outlet, a moose and her calf stood in marshy ground against a growth of thin pines and brush.

View of Pintler Lake from campground
south of the Anaconda Pintler Wilderness

The creek from the outlet of the lake bubbled it's way toward the Big Hole Basin. Snow covered mountain peaks rose to the northwest, temptation each and every time they caught his gaze.

He continued on through a lodgepole pine forest, made a slight ascent and arrived at the edge of a meadow. In the summer he had seen beautiful flowers adorn this meadow which was covered with grasses. He surveyed the area and knew that this would be a good place to build a cabin the next year where the trees would add protection from the strong winter winds. The roaring creek in the distance still reached his ears.

He took notice of the animal droppings of white tail, mule deer and elk, also the droppings of bear. This he didn't like, but common to see. He moved through a grove of spruce and out into another meadow. He headed for the bluffs above. The wind blew up the mountainside. This was in his favor as any animal from the grove below could not smell him.

He led the horses a safe distance out of sight and staked them out to feed and returned to the edge of the bluff to overlook the meadow and tall spruce trees that surrounded it. He could see trails crisscross the meadow below. He knew the chances were good for these were game trails.

Soon it would be dusk, time for the elk to feed. He leaned against a snag with his gun close at his side. He took a chew and waited.

A stately bull elk moved from the shadows. It held it's head high, looked and sniffed. Sensing safety, it moved out into the meadow. There was a wide antler span on it's walnut brown head as it grazed contentedly on the tall, green grass.

Charlie raised his muzzle loader and aimed carefully. He squeezed the trigger, heard the blast and the elk was downed.

He walked up the slope, took the horses by their reins and led them to where the elk lay. After he cleaned the elk he figured to stay the night. He found a high, strong limb and hung the elk to cool.

He went a short distance above and tied the horses so they could feed. He started a campfire, sat and leaned back against a snag and watched the fire's flame, smoke rise and a hunk of liver sizzle over the fire.

His stomach ached with hunger. He reached in his pack, tore a chunk off a loaf of bread, and sat and munched it while he waited for the liver to cook.

Through the shadows of the forest his eyes caught the sight of a Blackfoot Indian. Charlie stood, shot a whistle in his direction and motioned a husky arm to come join him. A few yards later he saw the pony turn his direction. The rider moved closer, then stopped within fifty feet.

A cloud of smoke dimmed his view, when it cleared he sensed the stranger's gaze searching out the camp, smoke from the fire and the smell of wild game, he then strode closer. His pony tied to a tree, the Indian took his knife from it's leather sheath and sat cross legged on the ground. His fingers ran across the blade, checking it's edge.

Charlie shared his meal and accepted the Indian's knife to cut up morsels of elk liver. He tore chunks from a loaf of bread and handed it over to his companion. Around the campfire, the two shared tales in their own language of the wilds surrounding them.

The redskin wiped his lips with his sleeve, reached for a scrap of wood from the edge of the fire. With a curve of his thumb, he guided the knife blade as shavings curled and dropped at his feet.

Charlie intently observed his gestures, the way he noticed every little thing, a shift in the wind, every random call of a bird, as if he and the Indian were of the same culture.

A couple of hours later his friend rose and stepped toward him. His fingers handed Charlie a delicate carved papoose to give to his wife. Charlie felt a warm hand on his shoulder and looked up as he emptied the last bit of coffee and a few grounds in his cup.

His eyes squinted a smile as his friend mounted his pony. The Indian gestured with an upraised hand. Charlie watched him ride off and disappear in the forest.

He stoked the campfire like he had learned in the Blue Mountains and slept between the fire and the rock ledge. He had gathered tree branches to use as a mattress and slept on his stomach. As he dozed off he heard the lonely cry of a wolf in the distance.

Daybreak found Charlie in a hurry to get home. This was one of the first trips to the mountains since they arrived and he worried about Katie and the children. He skinned, cut the elk and packed it on the horses. He moved out on his pony and led the pack horses through the meadow and the lodgepole pines. He followed a slope that led him through an invariable tangle of dense underbrush. He cursed himself for taking this route, but it was the shortest way home. He figured he'd make it home earlier than planned and surprise Katie with an elk steak for supper. He fought limbs and brush, a job in itself, then looked ahead and saw a clearing through the brush.

His pony smelled the air, became wary and stepped from side to side, snorted, whinnied and reared up. Charlie did his best to control him, and thought it odd, his pony was usually calm and easy to handle. Just then his pack horses broke loose from the rope that was tied to his saddle horn. His pony reared again so high that Charlie flew off and landed on the ground. His gun flew into the bushes.

Puzzled and worried by his pony's actions, he still didn't know what lay in store. The horses galloped off in different directions. His saddle pony was gone!

Dazed, he looked around from his sitting position to see a giant grizzly standing on it's hind legs. The bear began to swing it's head from side to side and Charlie could hear the grotesque champing noise it made with it's teeth. He knew this was a warning sign before the attack He figured the grizzly had smelled blood from the fresh meat and was ready for a kill.

Charlie knew he had to move fast. He looked at the bear and he looked at his gun. He made a lunge for his gun and struggled to position it from his sitting position.

The bear charged. A puff of black smoke emerged from the muzzle loader and he made a wild leap for the bushes and windfall that surrounded a fallen tree. He found the log to be hollow so edged his body inside. He couldn't reload and he didn't know if he aimed good enough or not. He lay not moving a muscle as he heard the crazed bear growl, snort and claw the ground to find him.

Time seemed like eternity and finally the noise ceased. Gradually he slid the length of his body from the log and worked his way out between the downed trees, limbs and brush.

He leaned slightly forward, muzzle loader reloaded and searched the area with careful eyes for any dark figure which could be the bear.

He wondered if he would make it back to Katie and children.

Chapter 9

KATIE'S DILEMNA

Katie had looked for Charlie all the day before and he was still not home. It was the morning of the third day. She paced the floor. She hadn't slept well for two nights with Charlie gone. She had heard a wolf pack howl about every hour. She walked to the door and looked outside toward the mountains.

The sun had risen and showed it's bright warm sunshine against the back side of the cabin. Gradually the shadows of the cabin intensified and then grew smaller in size as they crept closer to the window.

Katie sat down at the table and continued looking outside while rubbing her weary neck to try and ease her headache. Fear crept into her mind as she remembered the intuition she had before he left. She felt she should have warned him.

Looking north toward the Anaconda Pintler Wilderness from corner of the Pintler cabin in the Big Hole Basin.

Billy cried. She changed and fed him, then rocked him in the rocker her folks had given her. She tenderly smoothed the weathered wood of it's arm and wished she and Charlie could have continued on with them. She missed them so.

She walked again to the doorway and looked north. This time she saw something move in the distance. She headed for her rifle, then watched as the figure got closer. She then saw that it was Charlie.

She ran with Nettie right behind her and met him as he rode up. She looked up at him with a hand on each hip.

Charlie looked down at the small dark haired woman so fired up that he half-smiled when he dismounted.

Katie continued to look directly at him and wanted to know why he was gone so long and told him how worried she had been. She asked what she would have done if he didn't return.

He turned his back and started to tend the horses and said he'd be in when he finished.

Her eyes welled up with tears of frustration as she headed for the cabin with Nettie. She felt he liked the wilderness and those animals better than his own family.

She sat rocking as if to expend energy when at last he walked through the door. When he explained what had happened on the mountain, she put her arms around him and told him of the feeling she had that something might happen to him if he left.

Charlie consoled Katie that night and the next morning forced himself back with the pack horses to get the bear meat. He arrived back home at dusk.

The next month Charlie cut the winter's wood supply. His team of horses were his faithful companions and could haul a large wagon load. He was grateful for these stout horses.

He noticed the ground squirrels had turned in for the winter, and knew the snows would come soon. He piled each load of wood in the lean-to next to the cabin. He figured winter would be hard, as even the mildest winter in this country was not an easy one.

The Indians called the Big Hole Basin, "Land of the Big Snows". They would even leave and cross over the Bitterroot Range into a milder climate.

Snow fell as Charlie headed north to the mountains again, but this time to set traps. The money from the pelts would buy essentials the coming spring. He set traps the way he had learned in the Blues and it seemed an ordinary task. Beavers were abundant in this land with many streams that ran from the mountain lakes.

Winter set in and sometimes when Charlie checked on his traps, Katie kept one small trail open from the drifting snow to gather wood.

The deep snows covered the bushes, ravines, and creek beds to the same level. It drifted into the shed and impacted between the wood. At times the wood had to be chopped apart.

The intense arctic chill hovered over the area silent and still. Only the occasional sound of a lodgepole pine that cracked and fell as it became overstrained from snow and ice was heard in the distance.

Charlie was home now except to check on the traps.

The evenings were long in this wilderness country, so Charlie and Katie spent much of their time talking about their future plans to build a cabin in the meadow toward the north. They decided the trees would add shelter from the hot summer's sun and the horrid unyeilding winter wind. Beautiful yellow flowers dotted the area and short stemmed grass covered the meadow like a carpet. Charlie had checked it, and knew Katie would like it there much better. Besides that, he could make it home sooner.

It sounded much better to Katie, and they planned the move with great anticipation.

After supper, Charlie walked over to the trunk and picked up his fiddle. He blew the dust off, tuned the strings, and started to play some songs he learned as a boy. Katie sat and rocked Billy after she tucked Nettie in bed. She enjoyed this atmosphere. She felt safe and warm sitting in her rocker in the middle of the wilderness and listening to her husband play the violin. It seemed to come so easy for him, and whatever he did, he made everything seem like it would be all right.

In the clear night, moonlight glistened on the snow's vast whiteness outside the cabin. The sound of the Charlie's violin echoed outside the confines of it's walls and across the Big Hole Valley's peaceful winter setting.

Chapter 10

TRIP TO ANACONDA

The stream was full as it bubbled it's way past the back of the cabin toward the Wisdom River. It was late May and there were still sprinklings of rain from occasional clouds. Willows had the look of amber even though new green leaves were emerging. The grasses were greening up. A robin jumped it's way across the slope from the cabin treating the family to a sure sign that spring had arrived.

Charlie backed his horses on each side of the wagon tongue and snapped their traces onto the doubletree rings. He told them that this time they wouldn't be haulin' a load. He rubbed behind their ears with callused hands. He said he was glad about the price he got for the hides and furs, they could feed on good oats and hay from now on. He planned to buy some extra tools to make the job easier to build the new cabin and barn in the meadows.

Katie glanced out the cabin window as she heard Charlie talk to the horses. She smiled and finished combing Nettie's hair. Her hands swept down her long skirt. She wished for a full length mirror to see if she looked worth a darn. She'd pressed her dress with a flat iron to make sure she got a 'good do' on the white collar and green ribbons tied at the neck.

Now she could buy some staples again and some material for new dresses and play clothes for Billy.

She wet her hand to brush back her hair and hurried outside.

They traveled slowly over rough, frost-bitten ground. The frost gave way to the morning sun. There were already bright splotches of shooting stars and bluebells that dotted the warmer areas. Ahead a sage hen crouched among the brush. Antelope bounded away at the unnatural sound of the wagon. The Wisdom River wound it's way in long, gentle curves through the Big Hole Basin. They turned north.

Charlie pointed toward the peaks to the west.

Katie wondered if they were the ones he climbed, they looked much too rocky and steep.

He relayed that he had crossed the area to find out what was on the other side of the range and what he found had intrigued him.

Katie could hardly imagine the mountain goats and big horn sheep she heard about on those steep mountains, but Charlie? She glanced over at her husband and then their two small children. When she looked up toward the mountains she again felt a tinge of fear clutch her heart.

The trail to Anaconda showed deep ruts of travel. Main street was a bustle of activity. Charlie halted the team at the livery stable. After he made sure the horses were well kept, he returned to Katie and the children and told her about the town as they walked toward the General Store.

Charlie tipped his hat at an occasional passerby, when a jovial man stepped from the shoe store and with surprised eyes shot a glance at Charlie and whirled in his direction. His greeting was as warm as his hand clasp was long and strong. Charlie introduced Katie and children to this man named Frank Rumble. Charlie and Frank talked while Katie checked out goods at the General Store.

Charlie told Frank if he knew of anyone that wanted to put in a good day's work, he was looking for a fellow to dig ditches for

Smoke pours from the old works in this 1886 view of the city

Jim Keefe's Original Hotel was an Anaconda original, built in 1883

Buggies stand in front of the Anaconda Stable at Cedar and Oak

irrigation. Frank said if he run into anyone, he'd let them know where they'd be staying. He had recommended a hotel at the end of the street, nice place, good food and reasonable.

Charlie thanked him and headed into the general store. Inside a couple old cronies played checkers beside a pot belly stove. Charlie took a chew of the Horseshoe Brand tobacco and headed over to get acquainted.

As they left the store, Katie told Charlie she had found her yardage, lace and sewing notions to pick up the next morning.

The town was full of activity as they walked down the street.

Katie noticed a man rode in across the street on thundering hooves and reined in at the saloon, slid out of the saddle and tied the reins to the hitching rail. He stamped up the wooden stairs with a tie-down holster low on each hip. Then, she saw a well dressed gentleman as he strode over in front of the saloon, offered a gentle smile to a prudent lady in an expensive low-cut dress, then tipped the brim of his tall hat. After crossing the street, they passed the smoke filled saloon and heard the click of pool balls and the clink of glasses along the crowded bar. Talk and laughter floated through it's walls.

When they entered the hotel Katie noted the menu in the fine dining room, Sirloin Steak-35 cents, T-bone Steak-50 cents, served with coffee, tea, bread, potatoes and two eggs, any style.

The adjoining billiard room was crowded and a lively poker game took place in one corner of the room.

A Chinese boy filled and lit coal oil lamps as they headed upstairs to the room.

Katie was amazed at what lay over the mountain from their tiny cabin in the wilderness. She didn't know this kind of life existed. She half-muttered to herself that this was enough excitement for one day.

Charlie, however, felt at ease but didn't take in a card game that night.

The next morning they treated themselves and younguns to breakfast in the dining room.

A young black man approached and inquired about the job, said he was looking for Charlie Pintler. Said he heard alot 'bout him, and would be mighty pleased to work for the man. Frank had told him about the job.

Charlie sized up this eager young man. He was agile and wiry, figured he could put in a good day's work. Didn't seem to have a bad attitude either. He told him to meet them at the livery stable in about an hour.

Charlie and Katie bought garden seeds, seed potatoes, staples and even a new kerosene lamp Katie admired. She bought material to make dresses and play clothes. Charlie bought supplies to help build the new cabin and animal stalls. Katie hand picked a dozen chickens.

Charlie cracked the buggy whip and they lit out as the hired hand rode beside them.

A day's ride later they reined toward a green hollow in a cluster of willows where they could see down into the valley toward the river.

Katie placed a haunch of venison over the fire and arranged a few spuds in the hot coals. She checked on the chicks.

Horses tended, Charlie sat on a rock near the fire. He opened a package of Horseshoe Brand tobacco and took a chew. He told the hired hand of the trips to the wilderness, about the many lakes, streams, animals and the trails he blazed.

Katie heard excitement grow in Charlie's voice as he sat there talking about it.

The young black man listened with intrigue and a wondrous expression crossed his face as he took in his stories.

Once again that same feeling swept over Katie that he must love the wilderness more than his own family. She felt he had an absolute sense of wanderlust the way he talked. She held her tongue but announced with a tense voice that it was time to eat supper.

They arrived back at the cabin the next day and rested up.

Charlie instructed the hand on the layout of the ditches. He figured if and when he sold out, his improvements would add to the price of the sale.

Every day was filled to the brim with hard, back-breaking work.

The hired hand proved to be a very good choice for Charlie. Agile and wiry, he worked without any complaints and did whatever was deemed necessary.

Katie worked in the small garden throughout the spring and summer.

Charlie worked steady and hard and with more experience felled trees for the meadow cabin. He limbed and bunched them. He threw a half-hitch on one end and a timber hitch on the other, then pulled them back to the meadow's cabin site. When he had enough logs to raise the cabin he notched each end so as to fit into the previous log. The blade of the double bitted ax sank deep and chips fell as large as man's hand as he continued on a right and left hand stroke. The smell of fresh pine wood enveloped him.

After the walls were raised, he cut smaller trees for the roof.

As Charlie guided the work horses back to the cabin site, he knew instinctively that this new move to the meadow would also be a temporary one. He knew that this was a land no person could ever really conquer. The wilderness was his challenge and if conquered, it became a challenge no longer.

When he reached the cabin site he placed each pole one by one on the roof. He added sod over the poles to seal the cracks.

Toward dusk of another day's hard work, he had finished work on the meadow cabin.

The weeks ahead were filled as they gathered their belongings from the basin cabin. Soon the family moved and began their new life in the meadows.

Charlie hauled more logs to build the barn and stables. The hired hand helped him haul downed logs to cut firewood. With the cross-cut saw they worked until fall. With the help of the hired hand, they finished by late autumn.

Charlie paid the young man and he promised he'd be back the following spring to finish digging the ditches. They bid good bye. Charlie watched him ride through the trees and out of sight.

Chapter 11

NUGGET ON A SHOESTRING

Charlie, deep in thought, sat on a handmade bench outside the cabin door. He whittled on a piece of wood with his constant companion, his jack knife.

He had noticed the grasses and trees were already golden in color. The air seemed crystal clear and a chill penetrated his entire body.

Katie stepped outside and saw Charlie, asked if there was something wrong.

He replied there wasn't, he was just thinking how winters can catch anyone off guard.

Katie was puzzled as she knew Charlie was not usually worried like this. She walked back inside and wondered why he was acting so unlike himself.

Charlie's mind wandered as he thought of this cabin likened to an island in the wilderness. There were many dangers that surrounded it. The children couldn't protect themselves. Katie, on the other hand, knew how to use a gun, but he still worried about her safety when he was away. The Indians around here were friendly enough, but he still felt a chill beyond that of the cold. He couldn't quite place his finger on what bothered him, but it made him feel very uneasy.

He shook his head as if to clear unwanted thoughts and headed for the barn to make snowshoes for his winter trips to the mountains.

The next day Charlie saddled his pony and loaded traps and supplies on the pack horse. He noticed the animals had started to grow a heavier coat over their hides than usual.

There was frost on the ground and crusty ice on the edge of the creek.

He bid Katie good bye and headed for the high country. The sky was gray and bleak. It seemed much colder compared to the year before as he nudged his pony to move on. He saw an arctic owl on a tree limb off to the right, then spotted movement ahead. He looked upward to see an Indian riding along the crest of the hill. He rode south through larch trees and up the slope to the plateau. They greeted each other and talked.

Charlie told him of the arctic owl and the Indian conveyed back to him it meant a bad winter. The extra thick hair on the animal hides also meant the same. The friendly Indian was headed to join the rest of his tribe in the Bitterroot Valley, they never did stay in this country in a bad winter. The Indian held his hand up in a gesture that meant good-bye my friend, and rode over the ridge.

Charlie dismounted and tied his horses. Ahead was a ridge he wanted to check out. He walked on foot and surveyed the area with careful eyes. He trudged up to another slope enraptured once again with nature that surrounded him. He blazed a trail along the edge of a steep cliff covered with a sciff of snow. Deep, dark canyons hung below. His eyes caught blotches of fresh blood as he came upon a game trail and stopped short. His steps hastened in pursuit of it's source. His fingers scrawled his week's growth of beard as he slowed and studied the prints. Chills went across his shoulders, but an inward thrill led him onward. The silence was heavy. He could hear only the beat of his heart and that of his footsteps, one, then the other over rocky terrain. His head cleared

Warren Peak from Maloney Basin.

Anaconda Pintler Wilderness (Courtesy of US Forest Service)

a sharp granite formation. His eyes came to rest on an unbelievable setting.

Smoke rose from a campfire. An elk hung from a tree amid a hollow.

Charlie neared the grounds cautiously when through the edge of a thicket moved a man, a good head taller than most men, a kettle of water in hand. Charlie noted this was no Indian, but a big strapping fellow with a handle bar mustache and beard. He saw the man's massive hands put the elk's heart and liver in the kettle of water over the fire. The man upended a fire log and sat down, spit in the fire.

Moose Johnson with gold pan.

Taken from book *Gold on a Shoestring* with permission of Jane Van Dyke (Photo courtesy of Theodore Hess)

Charlie's lips curled into a grin as he studied the huge lanky Swede and his crude camp site. He saw him get up again, stoop and pick up a log as if it were a toothpick, and toss it on the fire. His eyes caught a big gold nugget that swung down from the man's chest and dangle from a shoe string.

The Swede looked up as Charlie entered the camp. Charlie introduced himself, and his hand dwarfed as the Swede's gigantic palm acknowledged the handshake. Said his name was Martin Johnson and Charlie replied his name was Pintler, Charlie Pintler from the lower meadows toward the basin.

Charlie said that was quite a nugget that hung on a shoestring, wondered did he get it from these parts?

Johnson gave information sparingly, but said he wore it since he was a young fellar. Then he told Charlie that's where it stayed, right 'round his neck. Before he came here, he did prospectin' in Alaska. He was lookin' for minerals 'round here too, been hikin' minin' 'n trappin'.

Charlie told him he trekked most of the mountain range, that a man could live off the land. He told him of the bitterroot flower and it's edible roots. Said you could find them on dry rocky slopes and they didn't taste bad if they were boiled and removed from their husks.

Johnson replied that there was nothin' better than heart and liver from game meat, lest it be a bowl of oatmeal. Said that was about all he ate, stuck to his ribs.

Charlie told Johnson there was some mighty pretty country to hike in to, but to watch out if he went hiking up into those craggy peaks. Reaching that goal was rewarding, but there was always just one more peak beyond that, and then another. There was danger if a guy didn't watch his step. He noticed the Swede paid little heed to his statement so continued. Charlie told of a deep, dark canyon that hung below the trail on one such trek to a peak, a creek had tumbled over windfalls, boulders, and pushed it's way to one of the many hidden lakes. He'd stood on the high, rocky cliff in awe at the wonders of nature below, then turned to move onward. About that time he'd lost his footing in loose, rocky

HIDDEN LAKE is truly hidden in the Anaconda-Pintlar Wilderness, straddling the Continental Divide between Highway 10A and Highway 93. The wild, roadless area is home to Rocky Mountain bighorn sheep and mecca to backpackers and hikers.

soil and caught himself on one knee at the edge of the cliff. His gear and rifle swung to one side throwing him off balance. For a split second he was afraid, it was a mighty deep drop off down there. Struggling to his feet he slow paced his way, not hiking, not climbing, but crawling on all fours for a spell, till he finally reached level ground and arose. His eyes caught sight of dingy colored snowfields on southern slopes, their edges frozen, melted, and refrozen. A mountain goat stood out on a nearby snowy peak with the sky as a backdrop, a couple others stood below. Above the timberline, scrub brush, rocks, and not much else surrounded them. He paused to overlook lakes, meadows, mountains and creeks rushing to smaller lakes, the beauty of nature was unsurpassed.

Johnson just stared at the fire waiting to hear more.

Charlie continued on with his story. Maneuvering his way down was even worse, he thought he was gonna meet his maker more than once, as he tested his footing at each step. Loose rocks above deep canyons slid underfoot until he finally reached solid ground once again.

Johnson scoffed, although he knew full well what Charlie meant, he'd been in a couple scrapes himself hiking rugged terrain.

Charlie learned that this new acquaintance was a man of few words, but he trapped, mined and even hauled live animals to the town of Philipsburg. Charlie left the campsite with the feeling that Johnson was a loner. He headed back to his horses the way he came and mounted his pony. He spent the rest of the day gathering hides from his traps as he worked in a zig-zag pattern down the mountain. He skinned and loaded them on his pack horse resetting the traps as he went. Toward dusk he reached the edge of the meadows.

Suddenly a shot rang out and it came from the direction of the cabin. Alarmed, he untied the reins to his packhorse and let it go as he galloped at breakneck speed toward the cabin dodging trees, rocks and encircling swampy areas.

Chapter 12

KATIE MEETS SEVEN DOG JOHNSON

His heart raced as he arrived at the cabin door and quickly checked inside. No one was there. Outside he checked the empty grounds and turned to head for the barn. He spotted Katie aside the woodpile with the Krag rifle he had given her for protection. Nettie and Billy were at her side. He rushed to her and the children, and asked what had happened.

Katie told him she got the hawk that had circled the chickens for three days. She and the children had hidden behind the wood pile and waited for the hawk to appear. When it did, she took careful aim and the hawk fell.

Charlie breathed a sigh of relief and smiled at his family. Katie had lived up to his expectations, she could take care of herself if need be. She was a good shot, he knew he had trained her well and she had a good eye for her target. He told Katie he would soon be back and headed to get his pack horse. He led it to the barn and tended his horses and hides.

Charlie looked toward the cabin and saw smoke rise from the cabin's chimney. It curled it's way up toward the top of the trees to form a blue haze. The cabin looked mighty warm and welcome. Katie's lamp showed in the window and seemed to beckon him inside. He walked toward the cabin and Charlie felt at ease once again that evening.

Weeks passed.

Charlie told Katie he thought it best they stock up on supplies and pick up the mail before the winter set in.

A puzzled look crossed Katie's face again. She asked him why was he so concerned this year as they had lived in places before where winters were anything but mild.

She noticed his determined attitude as he slid his arms through the sleeves of his mackinaw, reached for his hat, and told her to just trust his judgment.

She turned and began to wash the breakfast dishes. She shook her head in confusion as she heard him ride off.

When he reached The Crossing, Mr. Lossl greeted Charlie with a warm hand shake and asked how he and his family had been. They stood visiting and Mr. Lossl's eyes raised when Charlie told him he was concerned about the coming winter.

Old building in Wisdom, Montana   (Photo taken in 1998)
The town of Wisdom was originally known as The Crossing

Mr. Lossl agreed, after Charlie told him about the extra thick fur on the animals he trapped and of the white owl he had seen in the high country.

He said he sure did hope he was wrong. He had to drive his horse drawn stage line through the valley again this winter. It was bad enough in any season, but winters were the worst. Bad winters, nearly impossible.

Charlie stated he hoped he was mistaken too, as he picked up his supplies and mounted his pony. He nodded farewell and headed to the Geary Ranch to pick up the mail.

After Charlie had left that morning Katie bundled up Nettie and Billy and headed out to a cabin about a mile away, she had seen a light the night before through a clearing in the meadows and thought another family had moved in.

She knew it would be nice if there was a lady to talk with as Charlie was away so much of the time.

Billy and Nettie walked along side their mother through the meadow in the brisk fall air. Their path led them through patches of greenery and autumn flowers. Dense clusters of lupines in varying shades of blue had been spared of frost in protected areas. Small twigs snapped underfoot. Chipmunks and squirrels scurried about to gather food for winter. They stepped over and walked around windfalls, a white tail buck deer sprang and leaped over a log and out of sight. Nettie startled as a noisy crow flew from a tree branch.

Smoke rose from the chimney as they neared the cabin. They entered the grounds that surrounded it and several dogs ran toward them barking furiously. Katie didn't know what to do next, dogs were headed right for them. Then the door opened. There stood a huge man with red hair and a long, rangy beard.

He called to his dogs, they reluctantly headed back toward the cabin and he told them to be quiet. Then asked if she were

Moose Johnson the woodsmen.

Taken from book *Gold on a Shoestring* with permission of Jane Van Dyke (Photo courtesy of Theodore Hess)

Charlie Pintler's wife. Said she'd be the only woman in these parts 'cept once in a while a squaw.

Katie said that she was Charlie Pintler's wife and asked if he had a wife.

The red-haired man answered gruffly that he don't need none, his dogs were company enough.

Katie turned away frightened and disappointed but did not show any fear to this man. She bid him good-day and headed for home. Back at the cabin she loaded the wood stove again and pulled a pair of Charlie's long johns, holes in both knees, from the rag bag. She took a pair of his mittens as a pattern and cut layers of the material from the long johns, then sewed several layers together to make a thick, warm pair of mittens. She tried to keep mittens made ahead for the family. Charlie needed them as he was out in the weather often.

She then punched down the bread dough and shaped it into loaves. It was getting dark as she took it from the oven. She filled the wood box and lit the lamp. By day's end she grew weary, tucked Nettie and Billy into bed, then climbed in bed and snuggled under the covers. The cabin was warm and cozy.

Katie stirred as Charlie stepped inside. The aroma of fresh bread filled the air. He sat down on his hand built chair, took off his boots. He said he got the supplies they needed and she got a letter from her mother.

Katie jumped out of bed, sat and read and reread it by lamp light. She then told him of the walk a mile over from the cabin. She told him of the gruff, red headed man with a beard. Then about all the dogs and how frightened she and the children were.

Charlie replied that the man was named Martin Johnson. Said he talked to him a while back in the mountains, but he just wasn't the friendly sort. Found out he would cook huge batches of oatmeal and roll it into balls. He deposited the balls along the trail so he could eat when hiking in the mountains. He had told Charlie he planned on moving further up in the mountains come spring.

Katie figured with all those dogs, he just as well move further into the mountains. She slipped off to bed.

Charlie took a drink from the water dipper, washed up and crawled into bed. She snuggled close just glad Charlie was home again once more.

But that night the howling wind awoke Katie and the cabin grew cold even though the firebox showed a bright red and orange flame. The wind seemed to whip and blow with a fury as she stoked the stove once again. She heard something crash against the cabin door. Was that the wind? She knew of some savage animals and strange travelers in the forest around them. Her heart skipped a beat, and wondered if she should awaken Charlie.

Chapter 13

THE BLIZZARD OF 1886-1887

Charlie and Katie awoke to frost on the edge of their blankets, ice covered the windows. Charlie crawled out of bed, reached for his flannel shirt and buttoned it with cold fingers. He pulled a pair of trousers up over his long johns, then his worn boots over wool socks.

He started the fire to get the place warmed up and headed out to do the chores.

Katie stirred, shivered and pulled the covers up one last time. It was so cold she hated to get out of bed. She heard Billy cough. She turned the covers back and crept out of bed and hurriedly put on an extra layer of clothes, then bundled up Billy and Nettie. She poked up the fire and added a couple more chunks of wood to get them warm, they shivered even by it's heat. She broke a layer of ice in the pail and poured water into a kettle. The room began to warm, water in the kettle heated enough so Katie poured some in the wash basin, washed and warmed her hands and splashed her face with water.

She cut slices of slab bacon and laid them in the cold skillet. She mixed up the griddle cakes with sourdough starter. Coffee perked on the back of the stove.

The door swung open. Charlie stepped inside, his two days growth of whiskers were covered with frost. He set a pail of fresh milk on the table. He spoke through freezing lips, it must have been some wild wind last night, said he had to move a large branch that had blown against the door before he could go outside. He had chopped a thick layer of ice on the water trough, was a good thing the creek was close for the stock, but he didn't know if they could get to it if this kept up. There was over two feet of snow, it was still coming down and blowing, a regular blizzard.

Katie heated rocks for bed that night.

Next day the snow lay four and a half feet deep.

Charlie worked a path to the barn where inside the smell of sweet grass hay blended with the horses and well-oiled leather.

November winds howled down from the north with a vengeance. During these violent storms it was a task for Charlie just to keep a fire and tend the livestock and chickens.

One storm after another ripped through the meadow. Finally on a December morning Charlie awoke and looked outside. The storms were over for awhile, there was a chinook, it was thawing, water was dripping off the eaves of the cabin.

After breakfast, Charlie headed out to check his traps.

Katie knew she could do some laundry and the clothes would dry this time. She made several trips to gather ice and snow. She heated it on the cook stove to wash clothes. Her knuckles scrubbed the clothes on a washboard. With cold hands she wrung each piece and in turn hung them behind the stove to dry. She scrubbed a few at a time, just what they really needed, by the end of the week she had most of them washed and dried.

Billy's cough wasn't any better, as bed time came it's tightness worried Katie. She bent down, rubbed a mustard plaster on his chest. She tucked the covers up around his shoulders and gave him a good night kiss. She was worried.

That night she wrote a letter to her mother about the weather, of Charlie, Nettie, and then Billy's cough. She questioned what her mother would do. She always seemed to know just what to do. She wondered how they were doing in the South Moccasins by now. Then she wrote of her loneliness. She hoped Charlie decided to follow soon. They were doing all right, but sometimes he seemed so stubborn, he really liked it there. She wrote that she did too, it's just that she got so lonely. A neat hand filled the page. She wrote small to get the most on the paper. Then she addressed the envelope, used the edge of a marker to make sure her lines were even. She laid it on the table for Charlie's next trip to the post office, which probably wouldn't be till spring.

After Charlie reset his traps he arrived home late that evening with the skinned hides. Next day he tended the hides and stretched them.

The flame from the kerosene lamp glowed, and it's rays diffused through a glass jar that sat on the table. Katie turned her head to catch a ray of flickers from the corner of her eye. Her brows, thin and fine, rose to peak as she turned away to return to her sewing. Her young fingers, weathered from hard work and winters, still moved with dexterity. Her lips thinned as she guided the needle stitch by stitch around the edge of the mitten. She was sure Charlie would be pleased, the mittens she had made him so far were so plain, just from scraps and fabric she had on hand, but his initial stitched on the back in royal blue would really catch his eye. Her eyes studied the curve of the "C" to see if it was evenly stitched.

The thud of the snow shovel at the edge of the cabin door told her Charlie was about to enter. Her fingers scurried scraps from her lap and tucked the mittens in her sewing basket.

She glanced up as he stepped inside. She reminded Charlie of the cutest little fir tree she showed him before the snowfall, the one at the edge of the path to the barn. They agreed it would be just perfect in front of the window for Christmas.

Katie finished the breakfast dishes, wiped her hands on her apron and glanced out the window. Her eyes widened to see Charlie trudge back to the house. Tree branches bounced with each of his steps, with one hand he clutched the tree trunk, an ax swung from the other. With glee Katie dashed to the door and swung it open, Nettie and Billy at her heels.

He leaned it up outside the cabin, snow and ice dripping from it's needles, his eyes smiled and his lips curled into a grin.

Katie dreamed of the trinkets that would soon adorn their wilderness Christmas tree. She scooped hot beans from the kitchen range into a granite bowl. She turned from a stooped position in front of the oven door, a pan of biscuits in her hands, to see Nettie scoot into her chair and Charlie tie a towel around Billy and his chair. She was so thankful for the December thaw, she just knew the Lord would provide them with a peaceful Christmas.

That evening she marveled at the miracle of the season.

After supper the aroma of mincemeat simmering on the back of the stove reached Charlie's nostrils as he shoved the door open wide and stepped in with the bushy evergreen.

It smelled mighty festive, Katie had just put some venison through the grinder that day, it would make the best mincemeat pies for Christmas dinner.

The tree stood on a sturdy wooden stand made of pine. It's empty boughs beckoned Katie that it needed some attention, and soon was festooned with gingerbread men, red and white bows, and flannel angels. Underneath she arranged pine boughs with dry cones she had gathered.

Through the cabin drifted the notes of Charlie's fiddle to the tune of Silent Night. She was so fond of that Christmas song. Her eyes grew misty thinking of what a silent night it was in the wilderness. Then she dismissed her lonely thoughts.

With a light touch of the last bow on the tree, Katie's eyes lifted and rested in Charlie's and she asked him to tell the children why they celebrated the Christmas season..

Charlie added wood to the fire, sat back in his chair and rested Billy on his knee. He looked at Nettie, her eyes wide, waiting for an answer, then at Billy, the age of innocence. He cleared his throat. In simple words he told the story of the Christ child's birth and ended with the thought that their family believed in the gift of giving, too, the gift of love. They didn't need big, fancy stuff to be happy. They had God and they had each other, if he found anything under the tree he would be thankful for it was the little things that had true meaning. And not just Christmas time but every day of the year. With that Katie read a scripture she had underlined in her Bible, then silence. Then she got busy, she had loads of work to get done.

Christmas morning welcomed them to a blanket of fresh snow. Quart jars of dried apples and raisins rested on the evergreen boughs under the Christmas tree. The mincemeat pie waited in the warming oven.

Nettie spied her surprise on a tree branch and shouted with glee. Her mother reached down and picked up a rag doll and handed it to Nettie.

Charlie explained to Nettie that her mother sat up late night after night working on her little doll. It was very special. She gave her rag doll a hug, then questioned where Billy's was. It was kinda hidden behind the tree. Fir boughs bounced as Charlie pulled a small carved wooden rocking horse from behind the tree and handed it to Billy.

Katie reached between the tree boughs and handed Charlie monogrammed mittens. She didn't get a chance to wrap them up.

In turn Charlie handed her a wooden butter paddle. He noticed hers was getting lots'a splinters on it, about worn out.

She drew the children's attention to how their father whittled it with his jack knife. Her thumb and forefingers smoothed the wood and marveled at how he got it so smooth. Then she glanced down at Nettie, who studied the hand stitched features on the face of her rag doll, gave it a hug, and ran to her mother, swept her arms around her mother's skirt in a hug and thanked her.

That was the true meaning of Christmas, gifts of love. The cookstove was hot, and it was time for some oatmeal and bread and preserves. Then Katie would get the venison roasting in the oven for dinner. At that Charlie licked his lips, rubbed his stomach, smiled and dreamed of a nice warm piece of mincemeat pie.

In January, however, the temperatures dropped again and the winds blew. Ice formed on the snow, it was unbearable to walk as the new snow blew in to cover the sheets of ice. Tree limbs were covered. Charlie looked up and saw many of the pines leaned vicariously. Tree tops bowed toward the ground more each day as ice formed on their branches.

Then it snowed again. The trees snapped around the cabin. The cold temperatures caused the trees to freeze and snap so loud that it sounded like gun shots. They continued to fall around the cabin. Devastation wrecked the forest.

Charlie bundled up and went to tend the livestock. The cold was so intense that it no longer fell in flakes, but in ice particles that stung the skin. Ice covered snow left the horses' and cows' legs slashed with cuts. Charlie carefully wrapped their legs for protection with gunny sack cut in thin strips. Even in the shelter of trees the wind blew with a vengeance.

Charlie was appalled at the sight of the forest. Trees that had stood majestically around the clearing now had taken on a forlorn look.

The temperature had reached fifty degrees below zero and frost stood out on Charlie's eyelashes and eyebrows. His lungs felt as if they would freeze. He fought to tend to his family and livestock. They were his major concerns as he headed back to the warmth of the cabin. He opened the cabin door and swiftly closed it again.

Katie replaced the old blanket back against the door bottom so the snow wouldn't blow in under it.

The temperature grew even colder. Even two feet away from the heat of the cook stove the arctic winter air left a chill in the cabin. Charlie hung an animal hide over the door and filled cracks and crevices with scraps of an old Indian blanket.

The family huddled around the stove day and night and fought to keep warm. Katie wrapped the children in blankets even during the daytime. The heat from the cook stove was their only ally.

Finally in March a chinook came. The warm winds cut the snow and ice away. The creek overflowed it's banks as the winter's snow pack melted away fast.

Charlie gathered and prepared the furs and hides for sale. He stored them in the barn loft. When he finally gathered enough to sell he prepared for the trip.

Chapter 14

BANNACK CITY AND HOME AGAIN

He talked to his team while be brushed tangles from their tails, with a kind word and gentle movement of his hands he added padded collars. He bid Katie and the children good-bye and fought snow and patches of ice and mud holes. The wagon rocked it's way through the pine forest and out onto the prairie. As he traveled along the wagon road he could see where cattle had frozen in their tracks. He had wondered about the cattle out here on the flats with no shelter except the willows along the creek. He glanced at the feed lots made of poles as windbreaks that the cattle had chosen for protection, but that didn't even help. He reasoned the cattle were already weak from last summer's drought.

As he crossed the bridge over the Wisdom River he saw ice chunks and traces of dead cattle floating down the river. He veered around boulders and potholes. Hours later he directed his team into a protective grove of cottonwoods, near a trickling creek. His horses drank their fill.

Flames soon rose from a blazing camp fire. Charlie heated up food from his grub box and sat on a log. His shins burned from the fire but the night chill sent shivers across his back. He walked over to his wagon and admired the fine load of hides and furs he carried.

He dreamed of arriving in Bannack City the next day.

Next morning he worked his way over a snowy pass and leveled off again. Thoughts churned through Charlie's mind of the bustling mining town Mr. Lossl had told him about last summer.

He passed wash gullies, dredges and dredge ponds.

He had planned to check Bannack City out before. He'd heard of the hundreds in fortunes that had been panned from Grasshopper Creek.

Forty-five miles and three days later the rattle of Charlie's wagon echoed off dark shanties and tents as prospector's claims lined the gulch. He passed miners on the road and men in scuffed high top boots trudged from town to their claims.

It had grown dark, amber lights glowed from a few windows in the log buildings at Bannack City.

He sold his hides, then stopped by the livery stable to put the horses up for the night. The man inquired where he had rolled in from. Said he had seen plenty of miners, but couldn't say he'd seen many mountain men.

Charlie told him his name was Pintler, Charlie Pintler from the wilderness above the Big Hole. He said he had hunted game and trapped in rough country at the foot of the Continental Divide, and wouldn't pass it up any chance he got. Charlie felt in his heart that it was God's country and told the inquisitive man so.

The man asked him how he survived the winter, said it was the worst one he'd ever seen.

Charlie answered if they hadn't moved up to the lower mountain area from the Big Hole Basin, he didn't know if they could have survived. He said they had some protection from the wind in the meadows, but even that wasn't easy. Every day was a struggle. He relayed that ranchers must have heavy losses as he saw cattle carcasses floating down the Wisdom River on his trip over.

The man replied that he heard some were going broke, he'd just seen a couple of 'em that were hangin' around town as they spoke.

Charlie asked where he might find a good place to spend the night, said the Meade Hotel up the street looked a might pricey.

The man said that the Goodrich House wouldn't set him back too much.

Charlie thanked the man and headed down the street. He checked in at the Goodrich House, then headed for a bite to eat at Skinner's Saloon.

A busy poker game took place and a couple miners and a rancher exchanged conversation as they played. The rancher had just bet all he had and wasn't happy about his last winter's loss of cattle.

Charlie sized up the group. He figured the miners would take the man for what they could as the ranchers were desperate and discouraged. The rancher lost the game, threw in his chips, got up and stamped out the door.

Charlie asked with a friendly smile if he might sit in on the next game. They looked up. One of the men replied that it was his money. He thanked him and sat down to a game of draw poker, jacks or better to open.

A typical saloon Poker game in the 1880's

The men ordered another round of drinks, but Charlie ordered coffee. They looked up and scoffed, but Charlie said he wasn't a drinking man.

The evening wore on, the room grew more smoky and noisy. After the fifth game, Charlie raised the bet and waited. The miner frowned, a cigarette dangled from his lip as he looked at his hand and then at Charlie. The other miner removed his hat, downed a shot of whiskey and leaned both elbows on the table. One miner said Charlie was just bluffin' and threw his money in the pot. The other miner threw in his cards. After a silence the miner spoke in a gruff voice and asked to see his hand.

Charlie spread four aces and a jack, pulled in his winnings and stuck around for a few more games. Half past ten he stood up. He thanked the men as he gathered his winnings from the table. As he bid them goodbye, he said he hoped to play them again sometime, got a busy day tomorrow.

When Charlie walked through the doors, one miner spoke and said that he played a mean hand at poker, but wondered where he came from, and what was his name? Just then the bartender served drinks, and told them the owner of the livery stable was sittin' at the bar and told him he chatted with the man earlier today. Said the man came here from the wilderness just above the Big Hole Basin to the north. That he was a mountain man by the name of Pintler.

The miner said that he didn't figure him out to be a gamblin' man, he wouldn't have bet 'ginst him if he were. He scratched his week's growth of whiskers and said that he was one fellar he couldn't figure out.

Next morning Charlie picked up some ammunition for his rifle and some Horseshoe tobacco at Graves General Store. Gold pans, nails, harnesses, and all manners of merchandise graced the shelves and pegs on the walls.

He took a worn paper from his shirt pocket. On Katie's list was Harvest Maid flour, dried beans, yeast cakes and Sloans

Liniment. He wondered if there was anything else she may need, then he spied something he knew she would treasure. The ruddy complexioned proprietor questioned who this newcomer, a mountain man, buying a lady's luxury item might be.

He told him his name was Charlie Pintler, from the wilderness above the Big Hole Basin.

The man answered as if he already knew who he was. It seemed the talk had grown overnight of this mild mannered gentleman.

His wagon readied, his team headed out and left the town of prospectors, ranchers, and businessmen puzzled by this stranger from the wilderness.

He headed for the Big Hole and it's rich greening pasture land. Half a day later he found a creek, drank his fill, watered the horses and moved on. Night came. He made camp by a rushing creek, ate beef jerky and fried spuds by a campfire.

Charlie lay on his bedroll under a starry sky but brisk night air. The low moon cast a golden path on the creek.

At daybreak he bent down and splashed his face with cold water from the creek, ate some leftover spuds and bitter coffee and moved out following the wagon road. He set his team to a trot and covered wilderness that had scarcely been explored. He neared the Wisdom River winding in long, gentle curves.

He smelled the familiar pine and sagebrush scents rolling down the mountains on the evening breeze and it stirred something deep in his soul.

He gazed at the silent, snowy mountain range, rode on through the shady, dark forest, then turned the weary horses into the meadow and pulled up alongside the cabin.

White smoke curled from the stove pipe. A lamp glowed faithfully from within. Charlie climbed down from the wagon. He threw the sack of flour over his shoulder and took it in the cabin.

Katie greeted him at the door and he told her he made a good sale in town. He had bought her something.

Excitement showed in her voice when she asked him what it was. Katie's eyes gleamed as she walked over to him. He reached under his coat to his shirt pocket and removed a hinged jewelry box and placed it in Katie's tiny hand. Carefully she opened the box. Inside was a brilliant garnet brooch.

She said it was beautiful then turned and tilted it, and the lamp light caught it's deep red glow. Her heart gave a little flutter, she looked up at her husband and smiled sweetly, then back to the brooch. She asked how he knew just the color she liked.

Charlie just smiled. He said he had to go unload the wagon, he'd bring in the groceries and put the team away, then he'd be back to tell her about Bannack City.

She walked over and sat on the edge of the bed and held the precious brooch. Tears of joy trickled down her cheeks at his thoughtfulness. Then she wondered when she'd wear it, but knew it would make a nice keepsake.

****

Charlie and Katie had just sat down for supper when a rider approached. Charlie opened the door as his young black friend dismounted with a wide smile. He quickly approached Charlie who smiled and welcomed him back.

The young man said it was shore nice to see them again and after the last winter wondered if he ever he would, beings it was such a bad winter and all.

Charlie told him he thought of him out working on the range, too. Figured it must have been mighty bad out there.

He joined the family for supper. He had developed a kinship with Charlie. They talked about the bad winter of 1886 and 1887. He told Charlie that starving cattle roamed through the street bawling, many had staggered and collapsed and died in dooryards. Some ate anything they could find, including garbage. Many ranchers lost herds and went bankrupt. The stench from the rotting carcasses in coulees and sheltered valleys was so bad that no one could go near. He had worked as a cowboy and fought the treacherous winter weather. He, along with other cowboys had tried to save the cattle, and many of the hired hands had died doing so. Their bodies had frozen stiff so they were tied to horses and taken back to the ranch houses, put in a snowbank until a chinook came. The ground was so frozen it couldn't be broken to dig their graves. He said he also saw cattle that couldn't move because the snow was so deep, they just stood there till they froze.

The hired hand decided he had enough of Montana weather, said he would head back down south after he finished digging ditches.

The spring and summer went much like the one the year before and the children grew healthy in this high country.

Charlie cut wood and the hired hand dug ditches.

Katie did the usual chores and raised a small garden during the short season.

Charlie scouted and blazed trails further out of his normal range. But never did he take time to fish in a special hole he always wanted to try.

The deep, dark pool of water below the creek's falls caught his eye and he'd never taken the time to try it out. He told Katie that afternoon he would add some fish line and a few hooks in his pack. Said you never know what you might come across so he took his rifle, just in case. He struck out through the meadow on foot.

The sun had moved over the mountains. The wind sang in the pines overhead. The creek ran deep and swift with the thundering waters plunging down from the snowmelt. Through the shaded glen there was such solitude, no hint of danger lest it be a grizzly protecting her cubs. Charlie dealt with his inner well-being undisturbed. He trudged over windfalls. He saw ferns spring from the edge of tree trunks and moss cling to rocks in the meadow.

Delicate flowers burst their buds through
a forested floor near Pintler Falls

He found the never ending beauty of this place indescribable. There was beauty even as he examined an old fallen tree with torn away bark, which was scarfed by years of vicious weather. He marveled at the endurance of these magnificent trees even as they lay without growing. In comparison, he marveled at such a minute and fragile outcropping of tiny flowers at the base of a tree. They appeared as though they were planned for this special spot as he kneed down and studied their delicate rose-pink petals. He arose, his boots dodged puddles and mud.

Charlie swung one end of a log to the other side of a trickling creek to walk across. His journey through this nature land continued, his breath caught in his throat when from above the heights the rushing creek rolled around windfalls and blue-green water tumbled over rocks. As he neared the falls a steady roar reached his ears. The swift water fell below the falls forming white foam around the boulders before it sped on down the mountain. He stood on the creek bank and felt the spray of the cold mist reach his face.

He leaned his rifle against a lodge pole pine, took his jack knife from his pocket and cut a sturdy willow branch. He rigged up a makeshift pole, figured the hook and line would do just fine. There was always bait around if you knew what to look for, and he managed to find earth worms in the soggy creek bank. Wasn't long and Charlie's fish line dropped down in the deep, dark hole below the thundering falls. He could hear the water rush below, but his gaze never left his line.

Chipmunks skittered across the tops of damp stones, pine squirrels frisked in the overhanging branches.

He felt a bite, his pole bent, then nothing. Then came another, only stronger. He waited patiently. Then slowly pulled the line in and landed a nice cutthroat trout. A couple hours later the air chilled, Charlie stood, and gathered up his gear. He had caught enough fish for breakfast.

Pintler Creek in the Anaconda Pintler Wilderness

When he headed from the creek, he stopped to watch a lively family of marmots that lived in the thirty foot rock bluffs on one side of the falls. They had burrowed within the wall and had channeled tunnels to above ledges. He marveled at their well adapted way of survival.

He headed back down through the meadow toward home.

The hired hand had finished the ditches in the basin. Charlie paid him and he headed back to his southern homeland. Said he had enough of this country after last winter, he was going back home.

The family settled in again for the coming winter with an adequate wood supply.

Chapter 15

CHARLIE FACES A MAJOR CONFLICT

Charlie sensed an uneasiness in Katie and dismissed it as loneliness for her family. At the breakfast table one morning he noticed she barely touched her food.

He asked her if there was a problem and she answered she was sure she was expecting another baby.

She told him she would not stay here to bear another child in the wilds of the wilderness. She said no other family was around, she was here alone most of the time.

Charlie tried to console her, but nothing he said made a difference.

She told Charlie that when he was away, she sat, watched and waited for the sun to rise and show on the dirt floor. Then she knew that there was life outside the one room cabin. When the children awoke, she was happy, they were her company. She and the children would walk together outdoors and enjoy the wilderness, but for the most part, she was so lonesome for someone to talk to. She told him she loved children, but there could also be problems with childbirth. She would not have another child in this wilderness under such primitive conditions.

Again Charlie wrestled with his lifelong conflict, his family or his sense of wanderlust. He lay awake many nights. He still did not want to accept what he was told.

The wilderness had become his home where he had developed a strong sense of belonging to a bigger part of nature than he ever dreamed possible when he was younger. He felt it in his body and soul. He wrestled with the conflict of leaving. His family was much more important to him than the wilderness, but on the other hand he wondered how he could live and carry on without it, it was his solace.

In February he made a difficult trek to The Crossing to sell a load of wood. He told Frank that he planned to sell his improvements in the basin by springtime. He pointed out the dandy meadow, rushing creek, wild game right out the back door, and miles of blazed trails. He had blazed them himself and would like to blaze more, but he said life has a way of always changing.

Frank said he hated to see him leave, after all, he'd become a landmark 'round the area and who would fill his place to tell those stories about that rugged high country?

Charlie choked back his emotions when he replied that the little woman had put up with more than her share already, said that now that she's expectin' a little one they best move on. He told of his plans in the South Moccasin Mountains and his voice lifted a bit and a faint ray of hope gleamed from his eyes.

Frank studied Charlie as he spoke, he had grown to know him well and knew this decision tore him apart.

He asked Frank if he knew anyone that might be interested. Frank replied that he may be interested, he'd be out tomorrow and take a look around.

At that Charlie tipped his hat and rode out of town headed back to the meadow cabin.

In late spring Frank Rumble bought Charlie's improvements and took over the one hundred twenty acre parcel of wilderness property.

Charlie and Katie loaded the wagon with all the possessions it would hold and departed from the valley of the Big Hole.

ANACONDA PINTLAR WILDERNESS
DEERLODGE BITTERROOT BEAVERHEAD NATIONAL FORESTS
MONTANA

Existing Mainline Trail System......

✻ Thompson Creek, East Fork of Thompson Creek, and Plimpton Creek Portals are closed to public access -- Portals are on private land.

Charlie was silent as he traveled the familiar roadway and left the wilderness setting. He refused to look back, his mind tried to grasp what lay ahead. His team and jolting wagon worked their way through mudholes and around boulders northeast toward Big Timber.

Chapter 16

OFF TO JUDITH BASIN

Brilliant orange sunsets ended sunny days.

They traveled north across the Musselshell River. Over miles of rolling prairie, they stopped for vittles, camped at night, then moved on.

Dark thunder heads hovered over them at times throwing furious, luminous lightning toward the ground not waiting for the thunder to roll before another lightning streak.

Near Harlowtown they saw herds of antelope feed on the open prairies.

A few weeks later they crossed the Judith River. Charlie pointed out the Little Belt Mountains to the west and The Big Snowy Mountains to the east.

The mountains looked fingertip close, but they were miles away.

They moseyed along through the Judith Basin. They neared Rock Creek Bench, about twenty five miles west of Lewistown, then followed a lush meadow and crossed Rock Creek. Across streams and over benches the wagon took them to Beaver Creek.

A day later miles and miles of cottonwood edged a winding creek toward the Judith River.

Again in late afternoon, rolling dark thunder clouds hovered over them, thunder rolled, and chain lightning spread across the open sky. Rain pelted the horses, wagon, and everything in it. But as suddenly as it began the rain let up and gave way to sunny skies.

Mud was axle deep as they lumbered into Lewistown, the ranch supply center of the Judith Basin. A few buildings were scattered along Spring Creek just outside of town.

As they entered town, a faded gray mercantile store, a couple hotels, rooming houses and a log saloon lined the rutted street.

Charlie noted the livery barn and shook hands with a hostler ambling in front. He found it was a friendly village, with lots of cowhands. He could see why, it was prime cattle country.

A few Blackfoot Indians around seemed friendly enough.

The next day Charlie directed the team out of town South Moccasin Bound and crossed Big Spring Creek. He pointed to the east to the Judith Mountains, to Maiden and Giltedge, thriving gold and silver mining towns. Northwest the wagon took them along Spring Creek toward the Dundom ranch.

At the end of the second day the sun dipped below the mountains and a brilliant orange enveloped the horizon, a breathtaking sunset. A huge horse and cattle ranch came into view, in the distance was the Dundom home site. They followed a winding road, then Charlie directed the team through a pole gate and rolled to a halt by the log farm house.

Through the doorway of the horse barn stepped Katie's father. His frame was as big and strong as they remembered. He smiled broadly, walked over to Charlie whose mighty handshake told him that young fellow had been through some rough places since he last saw him and added that he was surprised to get Katie's letter that they were on their way. He didn't expect that mountain man to ever get his fill of blazing trails.

Charlie laughed back that he didn't get his fill, he could sure tell some stories about the Big Hole Country and the wilderness,

The Dundom farm house in South Moccasin Mountains near Lewistown, Montana William and Kate on porch, Pete, the hired hand, Mary Sherman, Mary and Fanny Dundom on horseback. (Photo courtesy of John Ihde)

and there were mountains around the Judith Basin country, he just may not be through yet.

That evening around the farm kitchen table Charlie, Katie, Nettie and William once again shared happenings of the last three years with the Dundoms. Charlie learned that William's horse and cattle ranch had grown immensely. The rich grasses in the Judith Basin had given him a good spread, quite a herd at that.

Next morning they arose early, Charlie was eager to look over the Dundom ranch. He helped William with the farm chores and was impressed that he had bought up more acreage all along. He had made it to the South Moccasins with only about half the ponies they had when they left Asotin, from then on he'd increased the horse ranch. On the spot he gave Charlie an offer he couldn't refuse.

Charlie and Katie moved onto a small farm over toward Spring Creek. He farmed, mended fences, cut wood, and branded cattle.

Katie at last lived close to neighbors, some were Indian ladies. They shared visits, recipes, and home remedies. An Indian lady told her of medicinal herbs in this part of the country and how she believed in them.

Nettie and Billy played with other children their age, a far cry from their life in the wilderness.

On August 24, 1888, another son, Charles Austin was born.

Life on the farm went on as usual, a busy family with a new beginning.

Charlie rode west one day to a neighboring ranch. He found quite a gathering of wranglers there. He sat on corral fences and watched wranglers break wild horses, bust their wild spirits with lariat and spurs. He made acquaintance with ranchers and spun yarns, took in all the braggin' and tough talk.

The sun dipped low in the Indian summer sky on his return home, he reined in toward the corral and dismounted. He undid the cinch, pulled the saddle free, dropped it over the top rail of the fence. He touched the velvet nose of his pony and removed the bridle and headed for the house, another day of life on the farm.

Time passed.

Chapter 17

JOYS AND TRAGEDIES

A baby boy, Arthur, was born three years later in 1891. Katie's mother took charge of the household chores until Katie was able to take over, then returned home to the South Moccasins and her family.

Late morning Katie stepped outside. She carried a basket of laundered clothes across the yard, spurts of spring's new grasses covered the ground. Johnny jump ups dotted the landscape. A few bitterroots had just burst their petals through the earth to the rays of the sun. A wisp of hair fell below her bonnet, the breeze tossed it in the air. With chapped hands she picked up each garment, shook the wrinkles out with a snap and pinned them to the clothes line.

A meadowlark whistled a sweet note from the fence post as if it was directed especially to her. Hand hemmed diapers soon filled the clothes line, the breeze told her they would be dry in no time. She was so thankful to be here, she remembered so well when she had to drape clothes here and there around the wagon to dry in the Big Hole Basin after Billy was born.

A burst of joy flashed over her as she passed Nettie, Billy and Charles as they played in the doorway. She hastened back inside to baby Arthur.

In August on his next trip to Lewistown word reached Charlie that his mother, Eliza, had passed away back in Dayton, Washington. He finished business, then returned home and shared the sad news with Katie.

He watched Katie cradle Arthur in the curve of her arm, then his mind turned to his mother. He told Katie he never saw it fail, the Lord gives us a life, and takes one away.

****

Summer and fall passed and snow once again covered the ground.

Winter was at it's worst. Katie was about a month from the expected date of her next baby. She chucked more wood in, and a shivering chill went over her body. A pain gripped her, then let up. She went ahead with the morning's work.

Charlie worked outside, but when the sudden storm came up stepped indoors. He dusted snow from his sleeves and remarked at how bad the blizzard and freezing winds had become.

Katie looked out the window, could barely see the shed, drifts were piled high against the buildings and sifted in around the window frames. She grew afraid for Nettie and Billy at the school house about a mile away and pleaded with Charlie to bring them home from the awful blizzard.

He fought the blinding storm to go rescue Nettie and Billy.

Her pains did not go away, yet it was too early for her baby. Katie endured storms in the wilderness much worse, yet this time she imagined them lost or frozen in the snowdrifts. She paced the floor, wrung her hands and waited her family's return. Wind whipped through the cracks.

Finally Charlie returned. Katie looked out the window and barely made out two little figures scrunched together on the wagon seat next to their father. She hurried to the door and questioned with fearful eyes how he found them. They had been safe inside a building, Charlie thought it best to wait for the storm to let up.

Katie, panic stricken, continued to have pains from time to time that day. Into the night they became more severe.

Charlie headed out and hooked up the team, fought the wind and snowdrifts, and struck out to get help. A kindly neighbor returned with him to help out. He had learned one thing about these Montana folks, when needed they'd help you at the drop of a hat.

Later that night, February 14, 1894, a baby boy was born, so tiny he needed the constant warmth of Katie's body. As she cuddled the tiny bundle next to her breast she asked Charlie what he thought about Valentine for a name. They would call him Val for short.

Faithfully Katie protected him from the cold, if he could just make it through the cold spell, by coming spring he'd be stronger. Steadfastly she cared for Val, but within the year Charlie and Katie lost their little Valentine.

The usual glory of springtime was non-existent to Katie. Sorrow and emptiness filled her heart. Nettie was at her side, cared for her little brothers, cooked along side her mother and calmly endured the loss of Baby Val.

Charlie was saddened, too, but reminded her that the Lord gave them life and He took it away, they must go on. He consoled her with a warm hug. They had others that needed care, spring was a time of new beginning.

He reached for his jacket, slipped his hat on and closed the door behind him.

That summer they raised a bountiful garden, Katie and Nettie canned vegetables and fruits. They picked wild chokecherries that graced the area on tall bushes. Katie made syrup and canned chokecherry juice for jelly. Charlie filled the potato bin in the root cellar, butchered beef and pork for winter.

A smallpox epidemic swept through town the winter of 1896, nearly everyone in the family was stricken. Katie was down in bed, so ill that Charlie rode to summon the town doctor. When he and the doctor returned they hastened inside to Katie's bed. The doctor informed Charlie outside the bedroom door that Katie was very weak. He thought she would be all right, she was dehydrated and needed fluids. He had massaged her limbs with salt to stimulate the circulation, not much else he could do. He'd seen many cases that winter, just hoped she didn't take a relapse.

Charlie thanked him. He had never seen Katie that sick before.

Doc slipped his arms through the sleeves of his long fur coat and picked up his black bag. He had another house call to make, the epidemic had kept him on the road all winter. Charlie followed the doctor out.

Fourteen year old Nettie had nearly recovered from the smallpox. She brought her mother a cup of rosehip tea and a fresh glass of water. It would help if she could just sip it. Nettie said she felt better, she would make chokecherry jelly, and reminded her mother of the day they picked the berries the summer before. Katie remembered very well how Nettie helped her.

The lid snapped as Nettie opened the jar and poured the juice in a kettle. She told her mother she needed to get an armload of wood for the cookstove, that her father was out doing chores. Before she left the bedroom Katie reminded her in a weak voice, to be sure and bundle up, she still had a cough.

That night Nettie developed a high fever with pneumonia. She went into delirium. Charlie struck out for the doctor, but when they returned fourteen year old Nettie had died.

Katie forced herself from bed, with unsure steps worked her way to the kitchen where she found a jelly stained kettle, wooden spoon, and glasses of home made chokecherry jelly.

Charlie had always comforted Katie before, but this was almost more than either of them could bear.

Charlie made a wooden casket while Katie, still recuperating, lined it with material she had sewn together with a single needle and thread. Tears fell on the fabric. She had to stop at intervals to wipe her eyes and calm her shaking hands. Every stitch was done with as much precision as she could muster.

Charlie dug the grave with sadness, despair and anger for having lost the precious girl he loved so much. Together they buried their daughter, Nettie, in a field near their home on Beaver Creek.

Charlie grew silent as he went about each day and tended farm chores.

Katie tried to keep up with the work but many times that spring the boys found her as she sat behind the cabin sobbing.

Billy looked at his little brother of seven, put his arm around Charles' shoulders and tried to muster up some excitement in his voice. He challenged him to see who could catch the biggest fish. They raced to the shed for the poles. They headed through the field toward their father's special fishing hole, home made willow poles over their shoulders. They fished that afternoon, but Charles got his line tangled, and Billy ended up with a makeshift hook and line. They saw big trout swim right past the line. They decided to snag one as it swam past.

Billy found a thin copper wire and tied one end to make a loop so when he pulled it would tighten on the fish's body. It seemed an eternity as they waited for the right fish to snag, Billy's arm grew tired as he held it outright.

Charlie shouted to jerk the line straight upward, there was a big one. The fish flew over their heads and fell on the grass.

Just wait till they showed their dad, it had to be fifteen inches long.

The two ran for home with the wire hoop tightly fastened around the trout's middle, with each wiggle it grew tighter. They ran into the house. Charlie sat at the kitchen table. Proudly they put the fish in front of him, smiling broadly.

Charlie looked at the fish. He could see a ring around it's middle between the fins and questioned how they caught it.

Billy confessed he did not catch it with a hook and line and told his dad the truth.

His eyes dropped as his dad replied that there was no sportsmanship in catching a fish that way, if they fished, to do it right.

Billy took the fish and headed outdoors without a backward glance.

Katie was cooking supper but stopped, headed for the door and called to Billy, but he continued to walk past the barn toward the field. She felt sorry for Billy, but knew that Charlie had taught him a lesson. Her eyes turned to the cross on Nettie's grave and tears again filled them. She told Charlie she couldn't stand to live at this place any longer.

Charlie looked up and she repeated she couldn't bear it anymore. Every time she looked out the doorway she could see Nettie's grave.

He said he understood what she meant, but they had to go on.

She planted a fist firmly on each hip, and repeated that she couldn't live with the constant reminder of Nettie's death anymore. They had to move on, they had to make a new start. She stood with her back to him with her face in her hands sobbing.

He choked back tears as he walked toward Katie, raised his hands to console her, then shook his head, no words came to him so he turned and walked out the door.

Chapter 18

GILTEDGE AND THE DEPRESSION

The skies were gray and low when Charlie left the house the next morning. He noticed a few pellets of rain as he headed for the barn to saddle his horse.

He needed time to be alone and think his problems through and find a new home for his family.

He passed many new settlements in the Judith Basin. The sky cleared and sunshine warmed his spirits. He rode along and took in the sights of this country, the fresh smell of the wet earth filled his nostrils.

He slowly scouted the foothills of the Snowy Mountain Range and found a spot by a rushing creek to camp. The sun set in hues of rose and golden, and in a small grassy clearing surrounded by mountains he tried to forget his problems. Once again he felt at peace with nature.

His spirits lifted every time he visited the higher country, it always had since he was a young man. He rode down to lower elevations and surveyed the country. He made camp on a creek by an outgrowth of willows. He lay awake for a long time and studied the twinkling stars in the spacious sky.

He arrived in Giltedge three days later and headed for Katie's sister and her husband's home. Their fine log and frame house stood with a backdrop of the Judith Mountains in the distance. As he rode up he noticed the large ranch with horses, milk cows, chickens and turkeys.

Charlie was happy to see Fred again, he had known him in the Blue Mountains and they shared many common interests. He told Elsie and Fred of their unhappy story and they encouraged him to move his family.

Fred offered him a job, there was plenty of work here.

Charlie learned that Fred hauled gold ore from the mines to the processing plant and also had his own coal mine besides the work on the farm.

Next day he looked the town over. He liked the looks of this little mining town that lay nestled just west of the Judith Mountains.

He located a suitable log house.

Once again the family left behind their memories as they settled in the town with the bright sounding name, Giltedge.

Katie and her sister Elsie greeted warmly and caught up on their family happenings.

Charlie and his family settled in and the next month the neighbors threw a surprise housewarming party for them. By two o'clock one fall afternoon, neighbors from miles around arrived in buggies, wagons and on horseback. Each brought their own special dish and the house was filled to capacity. After they ate, the women chattered as they washed the dishes and put them away.

Katie found herself visiting, laughing and enjoying herself again.

Charlie, happy and content for the first time in years reached for his fiddle, tuned it and started to play, 'My Missouri Home'.

Long, beautiful skirts swayed as couples whirled in time with the music. After several songs, Mr. Evans walked over and asked Charlie if he'd like to take a breather. He said he had played for several dances around the area and would take over.

Charlie thanked him and went to look for Katie. She sat in the kitchen with Elsie, her mother, and neighbor ladies. Charlie walked over, bent down, took her hand and asked if he could have the next dance. He realized he hadn't really looked at her for some time now, and thought she looked mighty good in her new dress.

Katie looked up at her husband, smiled, and soon they were dancing to 'The Ranger's Waltz'. He held her almost an arm's length away and looked her over from her high button shoes to the burgundy dress and his eyes came to rest when he looked into hers.

Katie followed his gaze and looked up at her five foot ten inch husband of sixteen years and thought that it certainly didn't seem that they had been married that long. His stout shoulders moved in time with the music and she followed his steps easily.

When the dance ended Charlie gently cupped her chin with his left hand and kissed her tenderly.

Katie glanced around and noticed a lively conversation took place around the table in the corner. Fred and her father, William, sat sipping coffee as they shared their latest ventures. She overhead

William Ira Dundom
(1838-1925)

(Photo coutresy of John Ihde)

Kate Vander Valk Dundom
(1834-1920)

(Photo courtesy of John Ihde)

her dad telling Fred he had been selling horses to the British for the Boer War in South Africa.

Katie felt happy and fulfilled for the first time since the terrible tragedies had filled their lives.

During the winter months Charlie helped on Fred's ranch and also worked in the coal mine to ready the coal for sale. It was a busy winter.

Charlie's and Katie's boys learned many things in the new part of the country.

The family planned a large garden the following spring, bought seed potatoes and vegetable seeds. Charlie showed his son, Bill, how to ready the soil to plant, then how to cut the potatoes with at least three eyes on each spud. He showed him how to dry them so they wouldn't rot, and how to plant them to produce a large crop.

Bill took in all his dad's advice. He liked to work in a garden. His dad counted on him a great deal that summer.

Katie was busy gardening. Bill walked by and told her she sure had a green thumb, she could put a stick in the ground and it would grow, then he slowly grinned and walked away. She turned and smiled at her twelve year old son, then realized he had grown much taller than herself.

The time had flown by rapidly without her realizing it.

Charlie hauled gold ore to the processing plant. He worked long hours and sometimes put in a ten hour day. He didn't mind the work but he couldn't help glance up at the Judith Mountain Range above town. His heart was still in the mountains at times.

Katie realized she was going to have yet another baby, but was concerned as the last birth with baby Val was so tragic. She didn't tell Charlie for some time. She was outside tending her flowers one day she saw some Piegan Indians ride up. She asked her children to return to the house.

Bill gathered his younger brothers and went inside.

Katie talked awhile with the Indians, then went inside and brought out some tomato preserves that she had canned the fall before. She gave the Indian woman the preserves, she in turn handed Katie something in a small bag, then rode away. Katie tucked the bag in her apron pocket, returned to the kitchen.

She had supper ready when Charlie came home from work. She finally got up the nerve to tell him there would be an addition to the family.

He walked over to Katie, looked down at her worried eyes and realized how frightened she really was. He gave her a quick hug and told her everything would be alright. Later that night, she lay awake and heard him breathing deeply as he slept, finally she fell asleep.

Katie knew she was almost ready to give birth. Her back ached, so she brewed some herbs the Indian lady had traded her. She seeped the pennyroyal herb tea each night before she went to bed believing she wouldn't have such terrible pains when the child was born. She was nine months and she noticed no signs of pain.

Another month went by, she noticed that instead of her stomach becoming larger, it grew smaller. She felt sick most of the time. But she told no one, fearful she would be scolded for taking the herbs. It went on for another month.

One night pains worse than she had ever experienced racked her entire body.

Charlie sent Bill to get his Aunt Elsie, when they returned he headed for the town doctor. The baby was born three hours later. The doctor stated that the baby was born stillborn and had extremely long hair and fingernails and looked like a wrinkled old man.

Katie finally told Charlie she had taken the herbs. The Indian woman had said she wouldn't have so much childbirth pain. She said she thought it would be okay.

They buried another child in 1897.

WARRANTY DEED.

Alexander Bower

TO

Charles Critter

Filed for record this 11th day of June A. D. 1898, at 1:30 o'clock P. M.

By W. Fulton

Register of Deeds.

_____ Deputy.

This Indenture, Made the 10th day of May in the year of our Lord one thousand eight hundred and ninety-eight between Alexander Bower, of Lewistown, Fergus County, and State of Montana, party of the first part, and Charles Critter of Gilt Edge, County of Fergus and State of Montana, the party of the second part,

Witnesseth, That the said party of the first part, for and in consideration of the sum of Four hundred & Seventy-five ($475-⁰⁰) DOLLARS, lawful money of the United States of America, to him in hand paid by the said party of the second part, the receipt whereof is hereby acknowledged, do by these presents GRANT, BARGAIN, SELL, CONVEY AND CONFIRM, unto the said part of the second part, and to his heirs and assigns, FOREVER, all the ~~entire lot, piece or parcel of land~~ situate ~~lying and being in the~~ County of Fergus and State of Montana, ~~and known and~~ described as follows:— The North West quarter of Section Thirty of Township Fourteen North of Range Nineteen East, of Montana Meridian in Montana, containing one hundred and sixty acres.

Giltedge, Fergus County, Montana, in 1898

105

In 1898 they bought 160 acres in Giltedge.

Charlie hauled gold ore from the mine and still put in a ten hour day.

Labor troubles continued to grow worse in the mines in a depressing pattern. The miners had to work ten hours instead of eight for the same pay, and Charlie did as well. He could hear the miners talk about hard times. When the miners had to take a wage cut, they went on strike.

The mine's owner decided to ship in some strike breakers to cross the line and wanted Charlie to guard the gold bars at the processing site.

The turmoil was felt throughout every line of business in town.

Charlie told Katie of the proposition. The position was dangerous, especially with the full blown depression of 1898. It was taking it's toll on everyone. No one had been able to buy flour for close to six months now.

Charlie told Katie good night. She said her usual prayer and fell asleep, but Charlie lay awake and considered the possibilities. He tossed and turned until morning. When he returned to the mine the owner approached him and said that circumstances were grim, but he'd pay him the same wage as when he hauled the ore. There was danger involved, but the bars had to be guarded around the clock, and he would arm each person who guarded the bars with a bayonet, pistol, and rifle.

Charlie thought about the man's position and the stand he had to take, then told him he would do it. He had to make a living for his family.

The miners grew more restless and angry each day as they did not receive any pay they had earned. The Miner's Union held a meeting and decided to get the gold bars for their pay. The others followed the cries of anger and frustration in unison. The angry group marched through town toward the processing plant.

Charlie heard them coming and readied his gun. He knew he was standing up for his life, not the gold bars. Many parts of his life's memories flashed through his mind. He wouldn't let a miner kill any that may be left.

They marched up and stopped ten feet from Charlie and said, "Pintler, we want those gold bars."

Charlie stood with his feet planted three feet apart. His hand was on his pistol. His eyes were ready for any quick movement as he replied, "Over my dead body, I have a job to do".

He stood there, looked straight toward them and never changed expressions.

The miners took note of his stance, studied his challenging eyes and knew he meant business. Disgruntled, they turned and walked away.

Chapter 19

LIFE ON BEAVER CREEK

Charlie, Katie, and family moved just outside of Lewistown on Beaver Creek among a protective grove of cottonwoods.

The depression hit families hard in the whole state of Montana and Charlie and Katie were no exception.

Charlie knew how he could make money for his family, he trapped and gathered furs and hides again, only this time in the Judith Mountains. This was a life he knew. He and his partner spent weeks at a time living in the mountains, setting traps and gathering hides. Occasionally he would return to town for supplies and check on his family at home.

Katie was alone with the children in the meantime. When Charlie returned one winter's day, she begged and pleaded with him to not go back to the mountains. It was cold, a storm was brewing and she needed him to be home. She pointed out the children needed him, too.

Charlie knew his partner counted on him but he did not return to the Judith Mountains.

He later passed his partner on the street and the man raised his head, looked the other way and didn't acknowledge his presence. He knew how this man would have felt, but he had taken the advice his father had given him earlier in his life, to weigh the consquences thoroughly, then make the decision. He had done just that. He figured his family needed him and his partner could make it just fine without him.

Charlie bought a freight outfit as another source of income. He asked Bill to help him on some of the ten day runs to Harlowtown in the heart of antelope country.

The dust rolled up like clouds around the wagon the first day they left Lewistown with a wagon load of lumber. Bill was excited and proud to be his dad's partner. The sixty mile trip was an adventure, they slept out at night under the wagon, ate from the grub box, and Charlie made his thirteen year old son feel like a man.

The whole trip proved to be an adventure to Bill as they rolled through the Musselshell Valley. Through torrential summer rain storms and scorching sun they reached the end of their journey at Harlowtown, nestled along the Musselshell River.

Charlie told Bill the story of when he was born between the Wisdom River and the Big Hole Battlefield, the closest town being Wisdom, when they were traveling by caravan through Montana Territory.

They filled their tin plates with venison jerky and spuds, squatted near the campfire, and he continued telling Bill of his adventures in the wilderness north of the Wisdom River and some of the scrapes he got in to.

Bill told him he sounded like another Daniel Boone.

Charlie said he didn't know about that, but it was a life all it's own.

That night Bill lay awake, his thoughts on the stories his dad had shared with him that day and knew he was in good hands.

Later that fall Charlie used an eight horse team and two freight wagons to haul wool and when a rainstorm set it in, it made a mighty heavy load.

While Charlie and Bill were away on a freighting trip, Katie went about the chores as usual. The boys had gone to school. When they returned they told her that a boy had thrown a rock and it struck Arthur in the temple.

A couple days later when Katie saw the freight wagons pull up to the barn she rushed outside to tell Charlie and Bill about Arthur.

Charlie and Katie became concerned when the swollen lump on Arthur's head enlarged. They arranged for the town doctor to see him. The doctor told them the swelling should have been gone by now, it had grown too large. He suggested that they admit Arthur to a hospital in Great Falls.

Katie and Arthur took the stage to the hospital. The prognosis was not good, the swelling grew to nearly the size of his head.

Katie was determined to stay near her son's bedside nearly day and night in spite of the hospital's strict regulations. She waited out the tragic ordeal until Arthur's death a month later.

Word reached Charlie, he and Katie accompanied Arthur's body back to Lewistown.

****

Charlie and Katie's faith carried them through tough times the next two summers. Bill took jobs at neighboring ranches. He took pleasure in new acquaintances. At the age of sixteen he struck out on his own away from home. He threw his knapsack and bedroll across his long legged roan and climbed in the saddle.

Charlie, Katie and Charles watched Bill ride off in the distance.

Chris Nelson, left and William Pintler, right
Taken near Forest Grove, Montana, circa 1913

Katie kneaded a batch of bread, dusted the flour from her apron, walked over to the window and looked out across the prairie. She brushed her loneliness aside and hastened outside to the chicken coop. Johnny jump ups dotted the edge of her path. The rooster perched up on a post and let out a loud crow. Chickens scratched in the pen. She filled her apron with fresh brown eggs and walked back to the house.

Charlie taught young Charles to play simple tunes on the violin. He learned new songs every chance he had from then on.

At the age of fifteen young Charles left home, and worked in the Lewistown area as a farm hand and broke broncs. He was nicknamed 'Audie' by his friends.

Silence fell upon Charlie and Katie's home but not for long. The next November they were blessed with a pretty baby girl who they named Winnie Cecelia. She brought renewed cheer and a meaning to their life as they had another daughter.

Around Lewistown their sons, Bill and Audie worked at cattle ranches, put up hay and broke wild broncs. Many a day they gathered for a rodeo, bronc busting or bull dogging.

In 1909 Bill headed for the land office in Lewistown and filed for a homestead patent on one hundred sixty acres in a little valley nine miles southwest of Forest Grove just east of Spring Creek. He later bought thirty four acres that joined his homestead from John Grensten.

Charles followed in his brother's footsteps and filed over the ridge in another little valley on Tyler Creek a few years later. They both worked to prove up on their homesteads.

Charlie and Katie moved again, they bought two hundred acres six miles south of Lewistown about twelve miles northeast of Bill's and Charles' homesteads, once again back on Spring Creek.

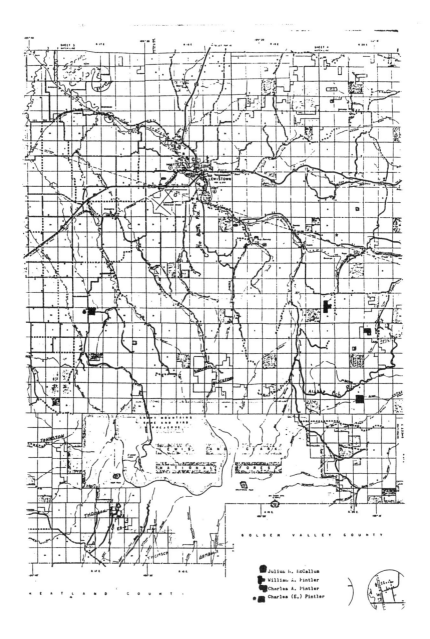

Acreage or homesteads in Lewistown, Montana in 1915.

Chapter 20

BY RAIL TO OREGON

Bill and Audie visited their folks often. They talked and shared events of the surrounding country. They caught up on new neighbors or the latest happenings around the Judith Basin and Lewistown.

They talked of breaking horses, of the spirited, wild ones that were hard to break and of being bucked off more times than they could count. All three had the same interest in horses and shared many tales that accompanied them.

Charlie took interest in his boys and their stories. They told him of a painter named Charlie Russell who they had become acquainted with, and of his paintings. Said they met up with him one day riding to a bronc busting venture. As they rode along, they came upon a guy sitting on his horse at the end of a road which led to a farmhouse. They wondered what he was doing, just sitting there, so they reined in and made his acquaintance. He held a pallet of colors and he visited while he painted away. They thought he did a mighty fine job, in fact the painting looked just like the country and horses they sat looking at.

Charlie said he had heard around about the painter, but had not met the man. He heard he was sometimes living in the Judith Mountains with an old friend, maybe trapping. He figured if his boys were impressed with the paintings he must be pretty good.

Bill replied that some of his paintings were displayed in towns around the area, and Audie stated that he was one feller that would be well known one day for his work.

After dinner was over, Bill and Audie bid Charlie, Katie, and sister Winnie goodby. They stood and watched them mount their horses and waved goodby from the porch.

Charlie remarked how the two of them had formed their own way of life around the Judith Basin area and how satisfied and pleased he felt about it.

Katie replied that she always enjoyed visiting with her sons, and said she sent some baked goods home with them.

Charlie, Katie and Winnie went back inside and Charlie took the deck of cards and spread them out on the table.

Katie washed dishes as Winnie dried them. Katie and Winnie chatted as they worked and Charlie was silent for a long spell as he played solitaire.

Katie glanced at Charlie as he played cards and could tell he was deep in thought. After all these years, she knew him well. She inquired what was on his mind.

Surprised, Charlie glanced up at his wife, not realizing it was so obvious. He answered that he felt he had done all he set out to do here in Montana, he told Katie he was thinkin' bout headin' back to Oregon, let the boys take over since they each had their own homesteads.

Katie told Charlie it wouldn't be the same, his mother and father were gone.

He said he knew that but he couldn't look back, gotta look ahead. He still had brothers and sisters there. He continued, this time they wouldn't have to travel by wagon train, they could travel by rail right here from Lewistown. Katie thought this offer of traveling by train sounded splendid, they had hard memories to live with here in Montana.

That night both Charlie and Katie dealt with the idea of selling out their accumulated acreage.

They realized long ago that the drama in the legend of the western rancher, was not reality.

Charlie realized in fact that he was just an overworked cowhand who rode the range under a hot prairie sun or endless miles in rain, wind or snow, to mend fences or look for lost calves.

Charlie was up at dawn, rode out on the prairie and drank in the fresh greens of spring. He told Katie when he returned that the alfalfa and timothy hay were coming up good this year. That was about the greenest he'd seen here this early. He said if they had a good summer, it'll be the heaviest crop so far. They had seen dandy crops before, then a hail storm would come through and knock it to the ground. He'd have to wait and see what the good Lord brings, harvest time would tell for sure.

After harvest time Charlie found a buyer. They arrived at an agreeable price on the property. The next morning they headed to Lewistown to swing the deal.

Charlie had picked the prime time to sell and when he arrived home he told Katie the crops paid off one hundred fold. He made a good profit and told Katie they could buy train tickets, travel in style and have plenty to get set up in Oregon.

They bid their family members good-bye for now, and Charlie, Katie and Winnie boarded the train for Oregon in 1915.

Katie's long dress flowed over a long knit underskirt. She smoothed her skirt and hoped it lay free of wrinkles. Her dark hair was pinned back in a bun. Her fingertips stroked it now and then in a primping fashion. She looked down at the garnet brooch pinned to her bodice. She asked Charlie if he remembered it, it had been tucked away in her jewelry box. He told her that's the one he bought her in Bannack City. He complemented her by saying it looks nice, and so do you, then he added, she always did like to dress up, had a liken to fashion.

He settled back in the seat, donned in a mackinaw and a Montana felt hat for the train ride.

****

They bought a house and property surrounded by timber in Gooch, Oregon. After they settled in, Charlie cut and sold firewood, fence posts, and logs.

Charlie and Katie (Dundom) Pintler
Gates, Oregon, 1916

William Augustus and Florence (McCallum) Pintler
Lewistown, Montana, 1916

He traded stumpage for beef. He cut, wrapped and weighed each piece of beef and sold the different cuts to the Gooch store.

Katie went about her daily housework, she and Winnie decorated their home, visited ladies and attended church.

One morning after breakfast, Charlie took another sip of coffee and looked across the table at Katie. He said he decided to ride to Stayton and visit his younger brother. When he returned he told Katie that his brother Wilbur was a fine dentist, but when he knew him before, he was only about eight years old. Later, when his dad died in Elk City, Wilbur rode back with his body to where he was buried in Dayton.

Charlie said that his dad and mother always taught them to set their goals and let the good book be their guide.

He smiled as he said they always gave their blessing. He said Wilbur followed their advice to a tee. He realized he was the only one who took off from these parts. Austin, Winnie, Ed and Mollie all stuck around Washington, Effie and Wilbur were here in Oregon.

Later, Bill and his bride arrived by train on their honeymoon in December, 1916. He had married Florence McCallum, who was eighteen years old. Bill and Audie had each sold their homesteads in Lewistown. Audie traveled with them to Oregon.

Charlie and his sons entered conversation on the years happenings.

Meanwhile, Katie inquired of Florence's family in Lewistown. She explained that she was the middle child, there were nine children in all, three still at home.

Subsequently, the trip to Oregon proved to be an extended one for Bill and Florence as he went to work for Mr. Miller, the road supervisor there that winter. Florence cooked for the road crew to cover room and board in Mr. Miller's furnished house.

The following spring Bill and Florence traveled to LaCrosse, Washington. A baby girl was born there September 7, 1917.

They moved on to Coeur d'Alene, Idaho in 1918.

Washington Water Power Co
Beauty Bay, Lake Coeur d'Alene, Idaho—a bay as lovely as its name.

In the meantime, Charlie and Katie sold out and rented a frame house in Gates, Oregon for a short time. Charlie visited and got re-acquainted with his sister Effie. By 1919, Charlie felt more at ease as he had renewed relationships with his family once again so they moved on.

When they pulled into Coeur d'Alene, Idaho, they recalled the hot summer day in 1885 when they passed through on the wagon caravan headed for Montana Territory.

Katie said she felt such peace that day and as they returned she felt as if they truly belonged there.

Charlie replied he felt the same way.

Chapter 21

RETURN TO COEUR D'ALENE

At the breakfast table, Bill poured milk over his oatmeal and said he was glad his folks decided to stay with them until they found a place of their own. Florence replied that it was no more than right, she said we stayed with them when we first moved to Oregon.

Florence packed Bill's lunch pail and he told her he'd see her that evening, maybe they all could play a game of cards. He headed to work in the lumber yard at the Blackwell Mill.

Charlie picked up his hat and decided to take a stroll down town, he winked as he headed for the door. He ambled toward Sherman Avenue.

Charlie liked the looks of Coeur d'Alene, he felt rejuvenated just seeing mountains again, he always felt more at home with them in sight.

Downtown Coeur d'Alene, Idaho, circa 1920
(Courtesy of Museum of North Idaho, Coeur d'Alene, Idaho)

The town about him buzzed with the sound of sawmills. He noticed a brisk trade at new banks, hotel, stores, docks and a few saloons.

He walked down to the docks, a steamer ploughed up the lake between timbered slopes with a load of freight. Varied banks, coves, and sandy beaches edged the crystal clear lake as the sun peeked through the fog. He inhaled the tangy mountain air, reveled in the nearness of the forests and the unspoiled paradise. The beauty of the mountain lake was unsurpassed. Once again he glanced around with an appraising eye at the majestic forests around him.

He struck up a conversation with an old timer who came to watch the boats come and go with ore. He learned that mining and lumber were the two main industries. They stood and talked watching steamboats come and go.

He headed back to the Fort Sherman Grounds to Bill's and Florence's house.

When he stepped inside, Florence was hemming flannel diapers on her new Singer treadle sewing machine.

Katie looked up with a pleased expression, she was glad that Charlie had returned and questioned what he found down town.

He told Katie of the changes since they passed through in 1885. Coeur d'Alene was now the scene of steamboats that hauled ore, gold, silver and lead from the mines around here and lumber from the mills, they travel the lake and rivers, the Coeur d'Alene and St. Joe.

Florence finished hemming the last diaper, turned and told them that excursion boats cruise up the St. Joe River to St. Maries. Her mother wanted her to go with her on a nice big boat named the Georgia Oakes, said they took cruises every Sunday. Ladies dressed in their Sunday best, many donned fancy hats.

Katie said that sounded like a nice idea, she also would like to make the trip with them.

Boarding The Georgia Oakes for a Sunday cruise on Lake Coeur d'Alene, Idaho. circa 1920 (Courtesy of Museum of North Idaho, Coeur d'Alene, Idaho)

October 3, 1919 a son was born to Bill and Florence. They named him after both his grandfathers.

Charlie and family moved into a rental house in town and in the meantime, he scouted around and came across some property three miles north of Coeur d'Alene. Nestled in the edge of timber, Charlie saw this parcel as a place of green magnificence. There were fir and pine trees and some tamarack canopied above saplings vying for the sky. He planned on cutting and hauling logs to the mills, there was plenty of timber on this land in Nettleton Gulch.

The small frame house partially hidden with trees proved to be adequate.

Katie fussed with the ruffles on sheer curtains to grace her kitchen window and centered a doily on the table. Her little touches here and there once again spruced up their abode.

Charlie set up with a team, wagon, saw, axes and wedges. He took off for the woods where he once again felt at home. He noticed a breeze sang in the pines around him. He saw chipmunks as they skittered across the tops of rocks and windfalls, pine squirrels frisked in the overhanging branches. The team of horses nickered as Charlie readied them, then held them in firm control down a steep trail as he skidded logs to sell.

Charlie felt young again as he worked long hours in the outdoors. He hauled logs for settlers and to the sawmills. He cut and hauled firewood for the steam boilers on the boats that delivered goods on the lakes and rivers.

Katie had just finished mixing up a batch of bread early one morning when Charlie appeared. She glanced up as he opened the door, his hand held a red handkerchief over his left eye.

Surprised, she asked what happened. He said a pine twig snapped and poked him in the eye, he couldn't see for the pain. He couldn't cut any more wood that day, maybe tomorrow. He forced himself back to the woods the next day, fought pain and blur, and managed to get out one load.

Bill learned of his dad's misfortune. When he had time off from the sawmill, he cut and hauled wood to town for him.

Charlie's eye continued to bother him for months, but he had to work, they needed the money. He decided if he couldn't cut logs, he could raise and sell produce and navy beans. It would give them some income.

He spotted a horse, Babe, and a buggy for sale. The horse would be perfect for what he had in mind. A gentle horse, she could haul the vegetables when he made deliveries. So Charlie traded his team of horses for Babe and a wagon..

Katie felt sorry for Charlie since that twig of wood poked him in the eye. His eye had bothered him ever since.

That spring Charlie worked the soil and planted the garden with Katie's help.

During the summer months they raised a bountiful garden.

The produce ready to sell, Charlie loaded the buggy and Babe led him to town. He stopped at each house along the way, and when he sold out, he would return for the next load. By fall, Charlie dried and shelled the navy beans, and patiently weighed and packaged them for sale. Again he went door to door and sold. Babe patiently waited for him to climb back onto the buggy before she took off.

Charlie's eye was getting worse, he could see only a blur most of the time.

He went to Dr. Sturges. He told him he was sorry to give him the news, but he believed he had a tumor behind his eye.

Charlie inquired what could be done for it.

The doctor said the news was bleak, there was nothing he could do, he couldn't operate. He prescribed medication for his eye, it would help soothe it.

Charlie was devastated. He knew what this meant, at times he noticed Katie looking at him with a worried expression on her face. He figured he had to remain strong, that the good Lord would expect that at least. He also would remain strong for his family.

In the many days that followed, Katie saw her husband as he came back from deliveries. He had let the reins go, and Babe guided him and the buggy home.

Charlie continued to get worse, so they moved closer to town. They put the property up for sale and purchased a two bedroom house.

Katie decorated the house to her liking with rich maroon drapes, couch and chair. The sunlight hurt Charlie's eyes and he had headaches, so Katie kept the curtains pulled most of the time.

He went back to Dr. Sturges again, he prescribed medicine for his headaches.

Chapter 22

JOURNEY'S END

The next day Bill knocked at the door.

His mother greeted him warmly. She told him she received another check from her father for seven hundred dollars. She said he sent each of the children an equal amount each time he made a profit on his dealings. He had also ventured in a new business as a stockholder in the bank of Moore, Montana.

Bill replied that he was glad that his granddad was able to help out and was a successful business person.

She told him of her concern about his father. He always did like to sit outside in the evenings, it was unbearable now because the light hurt his eyes.

Bill asked if there was anything they could do.

She said no, he went back to the doctor and he prescribed some medicine for his headaches, and he still used the eye cup with boric acid mixture, but that's all they could do to help him. She told him that Charlie was very independent, that he wouldn't ask for any help of any kind.

As Bill listened to his mother, he knew what he could do to help his dad.

He brought them half the hog he had butchered from over on Dollar Street. He worked at the Coeur d'Alene Mill and the first thing after work the next day, he went to the office and charged lumber to himself. The next week end he hauled the lumber to his dad's place and built a porch with a roof overhead.

Charlie once again enjoyed sitting on the porch in the evenings in his blue painted rocking chair. After the supper dishes were done Katie would often join him.

She planted bleeding hearts at the edge of the porch.

Charlie still worked what he could and added plum trees to the backyard garden area. It was secluded and shady in the summertime.

Bill built a shed in the backyard to store their tools and garden supplies.

A new baby boy had arrived April 23,1923, but that didn't dim Bill's senses, he had a strong commitment to help his folks out.

Charlie and Katie worked together gardening in the back yard during the spring and summer months, Katie canned plums and pears for winter and made tomato preserves, with her own special recipe.

When Bill visited his folks, Katie, Charlie and Bill reminisced about the life they had lived in Montana, both in the Judith Basin and along the Musselshell.

Charlie told tales, some they had heard for the first time, about when they lived in the wilderness and the Big Hole Valley.

Charlie told on one trip while in Montana after he had gathered hides, he bound them to a log, and stood with his rifle as a brace. He headed down the river. He was going along just fine when he saw an Indian friend riding breakneck speed along the bank waving. He said he waved back, thought he was pleased to see him. Just then, he spotted some falls ahead. It was too late as the log went end over end. He thought he was gonna meet his maker, but he was thrown into the air and came down on the same darn log. After making it to shore, the Indian wanted him to share camp with him and his squaw. He stayed and got dried out while the squaw fried greasecakes in bear fat for supper, They were so rich he couldn't sleep all night. They had to laugh at the circumstances.

When Bill departed, Charlie walked over to the organ and began to play The Old Rugged Cross and he sang along with the music. As Katie cooked, she hummed along.

Charlie played the organ more often now and Katie enjoyed listening.

That evening Charlie reminded Katie, they had three fine children that lived to adulthood. He said Bill was a square-shooter and honest as the day is long. He was the best carpenter he'd ever seen. And Audie plays the fiddle better than anyone in the country, in fact better than anyone he ever did hear. Winnie had helped out many times. He said he was sincerely glad that Winnie and Katie were close. He continued on to say that their children had grown into good folks. They had all chosen good partners when they married. All three of them picked mates that had high standards. They were all honest and hard workers and came from good families. He concluded by telling how proud he felt of their family.

Katie smiled back at him and agreed.

When he rested Katie drew the heavy drapes between the rooms so he could rest more comfortably in the darkened room. Later when she peeked in on him, he had a slight smile on his face as he lay dreaming.

Each and every time Bill and his family visited, Charlie told more adventurous stories of his past experiences.

Throughout the next two years, Bill stood by and helped his folks at every opportunity. He knew it would only be a matter of time.

By fall, Charlie was bedfast. Katie kept constant vigil.

The aroma of molasses baked beans filled the kitchen on Bill and his family's next visit. When they entered the bedroom however, they saw him as he lay in the Victorian style bed with a tall headboard. Above the headboard hung a picture of Jesus.

They were saddened as he was continually growing worse.

Charlie would still visit, however he could hardly see. He called Bill's oldest son over to him. The little five year old stood there, and looked nearly straight across at his grandfather as he lay in the huge bed. His grandfather spoke and told him since he was his first grandson that he wanted him to have his rifle. He said it came out west with him and got him out of some tight pinches. The five year old looked at his dying grandfather and told him thank you.

The family left saddened, and told Katie they would return soon.

Katie headed for the bedroom where Charlie lay. She pulled her rocker up beside the bed, and fed him bites of the molasses baked beans and the chicken soup she had prepared for dinner. He barely ate anything and she noticed he talked in a slower voice, she felt disturbed by it.

Charlie said that he learned long ago that in order to live in the wilderness, you have to live with it, but it is always the master. Then he told her that it was the master after all.

She told him encouragingly that he was the master on every trip that she knew of in the Montana wilderness.

He replied that it was the wilderness that ended up and got him.

She rubbed her taut muscles in her neck and thought that this was more than she could bear. He was getting worse fast. Her eyes filled with tears when she thought how much slower Charlie's speech was today, and he seemed to have more trouble remembering. She wiped her tears away, sniffed and straightened up in the chair.

She sat and held his hand as he started to mutter, his voice lowered, so she leaned over and heard him say, "when a man dies, he is like a fly speck on the wall, wipe one away and no one would even know it was there."

She felt taken aback but told him she would be back and wash him up, said he'd feel better. She returned with a wash basin of warm water and fresh smelling soap. She gently wiped his face, neck and hands, and he said it smelled fresh, like the woods, and then drifted off to sleep.

The next morning he awoke and asked if she was there.

She said that she was sitting right beside him.

He whispered that they had a good life together even though many times were tough, but said she had always stuck right by his side.

She replied that many times she felt were unbearable, but he stuck right aside her, too.

He said she was the best thing that ever happened to him and that he wouldn't have made it without her even though he never told her so.

She gently replied that she wouldn't have made it without him either and wondered many times what she would have done if he never returned.

Katie then realized how much she really did count on him and tears fell down her cheeks and onto her long skirt. She knew it wouldn't be long now and looked up at the picture of Jesus and prayed for her husband.

That night she knelt and prayed for strength again before she crept into bed beside him.

Charles Ellsworth Pintler passed away silently on September 15, 1925.

Epilogue

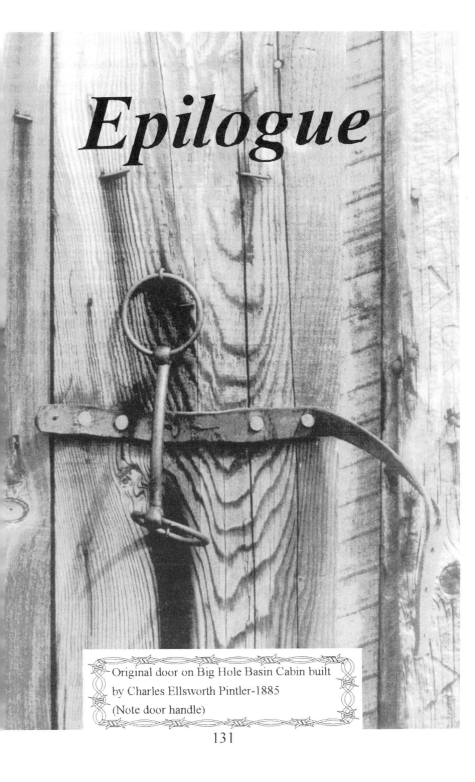

Original door on Big Hole Basin Cabin built by Charles Ellsworth Pintler-1885 (Note door handle)

Charles Ellsworth Pintler did not know that the wilderness he grew to love would someday bear his name, but he has left behind a legacy few men have equaled, for standing in majestic tribute to this same man is the Anaconda-Pintler Wilderness. There is also a Pintler Creek named from him that flows from the Blue Mountains in Washington State where he homesteaded. No greater monument could be given to a man who exemplified, as well as his wife, Katie, the hardy spirit of the pioneers who came before us.

Charles was buried in Forest Cemetery, Coeur d'Alene, Idaho.

Katie continued living at the family residence and carried on an active, productive life.

Over the years her narratives and anecdotes of Charlie's and her pioneer life unfolded. She revealed joys, she touched our hearts with tragedies. In her cunning manner she quipped personal incidents that raised an eyebrow or brought a chuckle. She was an inspiration to the last days of her life. She passed away in 1966 at the age of 101.

She was also buried in the Forest Cemetery in Coeurd'Alene, Idaho.

Katie never learned the US Forest Service had established the wilderness as the Anaconda Pintlar <u>Primitive</u> Area on October 2, 1937, or that it was reclassified in 1962 as the Anaconda-Pintlar Wilderness Area. She never learned that a Pintler Creek near the Blue Mountains in Washington State carried Charlie's name. Unknown to her, The National Wilderness Preservation System established the Wilderness Act on September 3, 1964.

The William Pintler family first learned of the wilderness named from Charles Ellsworth Pintler in early 1965. Relatives living in Darby, Montana had read about the Anaconda-Pintlar Wilderness after the Wilderness Act was established in 1964.

July 16, 1965, a son of William and Florence Pintler drove his parents to Montana. They visited the Big Hole Battlefield and Wisdom, Montana.

William tried to locate the correct site where he was born 80 years earlier alongside the covered wagon. He visited with an old-timer, Mr. Wampler, and shared early day history of the area.

In 1968, William Pintler's grandson worked at a local service station, when a lady from Butte, Montana stopped by. After learning that he was a Pintler, she relayed information to him of the proposed Senate Joint Resolution No. 16 to change the name to honor the late senator, Robert F. Kennedy. Petitions had been distributed in Montana at that time.

The Pintlers campaigned with letters to legislators to not change the name.

The name was not changed.

Again, in 1969, William and Florence Pintler and seven family members visited the area again and noted the signs were misspelled with an 'a' so William relayed the information to the District Ranger Station of the incorrect spelling, but nothing was done.

At the age of 84 years William camped and fished with his family at Pintler Lake. He viewed the mountain range, meadows, Pintler Creek and Lake, and primitive wilderness bearing his father's name. He recalled and shared memories of his father, pioneer and trail blazer, Charles Ellsworth Pintler. He studied the cut of logs on a cabin in the meadows wondering if that was the one built by his father.

William Augustus Pintler passed away in 1976 and is buried in the Forest Cemetery in Coeur d'Alene, Idaho.

On May 21, 1978 the first scenic route in Montana State, The Pintler Scenic Route, was dedicated.

In order to carry on our father's endeavor to correct the spelling of Pintler, historical proof provided by family members was gathered.

A granddaughter of Charles Ellsworth Pintler sent the information on to the Wisdom District Ranger, John J. Dolan about the incorrect spelling in an attempt to change the name from 'a' to the correct spelling 'e'. He in turn relayed the information on to the proper officials.

Months of correspondence later, a letter was received August 8, 1978 that the Board of Geographic Names in Washington D. C. had officially recognized the correct spelling. From that point on all reference to Pintler would be correctly spelled.

August 24, 1978 Charles and Katie's cabin was identified with the help of the same Wisdom District Ranger.

Sincere thanks and gratitude go out to the US Forest Service District Ranger, John J. Dolan, whose efforts, back in 1978 helped change the name to the proper spelling. Also for going above and beyond the call of duty in locating the original cabin that Charles Pintler built in the Big Hole Basin. It still stands today.

Martin 'Moose' Johnson, also called seven or eleven dog Johnson, lived in the wilderness for forty four years until his untimely death when he was seventy nine. He fell when he was returning to camp from a hunting trip eight miles south of Moose Lake in the wilderness area. He was crossing the face of a 150 foot cliff, 40 feet above a 300 foot talus slope. Tracks in the snow indicated he had lost his footing, fell and rolled to the spot where his body was found. He died on October 22, 1941. He was buried October 29, 1941 in Philipsburg, Montana.

These rugged individuals, Charles Ellsworth Pintler and Martin 'Moose' Johnson lived their lives at a time when they depended solely upon themselves when trekking these dangerous mountain slopes. No ropes were held in place for safety while climbing a mountain's steep, dangerous, snowy trails. No special shoes were available to prevent slipping and no special clothing protected their hardy hides from the weather. Yet, these men, and men like them have formed and created the history of our great country.

Charles Pintler was not well known, but the same trail systems remain in place today in the Anaconda Pintler Wilderness just as it did over a century ago when this early pioneer blazed them with only bare essentials.

"A good man needs only salt and a few matches to make it in the wilderness", quoted Charles Ellsworth Pintler.

Our search has led us through an intriguing adventure, and resulted in weaving research and stories we had gathered over the years into a legacy we feel is worthy to share.

From an Article
By Sally Campbell

"Little is known of this rugged individual, Charles E. Pintler, who helped explore much of this country," Vanaye Niederhauser, Forest Service officer at Missoula, Mont., writes. "He blazed trails for those who settled the West and he came to the Anaconda-Pintlar, Wilderness area in 1885."

Despite a spelling error when the region was named (Pintlar/Pintler) probably dating back to at least 1929, and despite records being scarce, Pintler's descendants have carried forth for us all something more valueable—the essence of the character of Charles Ellsworth Pintler.

A Window To The Rest of the Story

SENATE JOINT RESOLUTION No. 16

INTRODUCED BY McKEON, KEENAN, SIDERIUS, REBER, SHEEHY, REARDON, LYNCH, McDONALD, MITCHELL, McGOWAN, DeWOLFE, GROFF, HAFFERMAN, FLYNN, DZIVI, ANDERSON, GOODHEART, GRAHAM, NEES, BOLLINGER, MAHONEY, BOYLAN, JAMES, BERTSCHE, THIESSEN

A JOINT RESOLUTION OF THE SENATE AND HOUSE OF REPRESENTATIVES OF THE STATE OF MONTANA, REQUESTNG THE CONGRESS OF THE UNITED STATES OF AMERICA TO CHANGE THE NAME OF "THE PINTLAR WILDERNESS AREA" TO "ROBERT F. KENNEDY WILDERNESS AREA."

1 WHEREAS, "The Pintlar Wilderness Area" preserves a por-
2 tion of our state as created by nature and guarantees this area
3 to the generations, and
4 WHEREAS, this area has majestic mountains, cascading
5 streams and tranquil lakes depicting man's struggle within
6 man, man's struggle with nature and nature's struggle within
7 nature, and
8 WHEREAS, the late Senator Robert F. Kennedy knew and
9 loved the west and the primitive areas of the west, and
10 WHEREAS, the late Senator Robert F. Kennedy did meet
11 the challenge of nature; did climb the peaks of mountains; did

Senate Joint Resolution No. 16

float the cascading streams and did enjoy the tranquility of lakes and all of the beauties and joys of nature unmarred by man and preserved as God created nature, and

WHEREAS, the untimely death of the late Senator Robert F. Kennedy is such as to cause men of peace and men of public affairs to note how the spirit of man can move through life to death, yet remain as a symbolic and significant influence on man as created by God, and

WHEREAS, the legislative assembly of the state of Montana deems it proper to preserve the name and traditions of the late Senator Robert F. Kennedy in the same manner as the wilderness area, a place of peace, unspoiled by man and dedicated to the generation.

NOW, THEREFORE, BE IT RESOLVED BY THE SENATE AND HOUSE OF REPRESENTATIVES OF THE STATE OF MONTANA:

That the Congress of the United States of America exercise It's law making functions by doing all things necessary and proper to change the wilderness area now known as "The Pintlar Wilderness Area" located in the Deer Lodge National Forest area of the state of Montana and the Beaverhead National Forest area of the state of Montana to the name of "The Robert F. Kennedy Wilderness Area", and

BE IT FURTHER RESOLVED, that copies of this resolution be filed with the secretary of state of the state of Montana and forworded by him to the Honorable Mike Mansfield, United States Senator from the state of Montana; the Honorable Lee Metcalf, United States Senator from the state of Montana; the Honorable Arnold Olsen, Congressman from the first congres-

41 sional district of the state of Montana and the Honorable James
42 A. Battin, Congressman from the second congressional district
43 of the state of Montana, and

44 BE IT FURTHER RESOLVED, that the secretary of state
45 be directed to send copies of this resolution to members of the
47 family of the late Senator Robert F. Kennedy.

Senate Joint Resolution No. 16

Newman Lake,
Washington
February 11, 1969

Senator John McKeon
State Capitol Building
Helena, Montana 59601

Senator McKeon:

As you say little is known of Charles Pintler. I would like to inform you of what I know as he was my father.

Charles Pintler took a homestead in Asotin County, Washington in 1878 and married Katie Dundom in 1880 in Lewiston, Idaho. He and Grandfather Dundom traded their homesteads for Indian ponies. There were about 400 head in all. They worked their way by caravan to Montana and camped on the Big Hole Battleground on July 14, 1885. The next day they continued but had to stop at the place where I was born, between what is now called Pintler Creek and the Battleground. They then moved to Pintler Meadows near water and built a cabin. As he had used his homestead rights, in Asotin, he sold his improvements and moved on to Lewistown, Montana.

Charles Pintler was a man of his word, endured hardships, and did a great deal of hunting. He was another Daniel Boone in his way of life in getting along with the Indians as well as the whites. Although he did not receive credit for these first frontier days, he was one of the true pioneers which helped make the country what it is today. I think the pioneers should keep their rightful place as it is a part of the true American heritage. I would like the Pintler-Anaconda Wilderness Area known for generations to come, (especially his descendents) as it means a great deal to keep this true identity.

If the Pintler Wilderness Area is changed in name, I believe the Pintler Creek, Pintler Lake, and Pintler Peak should carry the same name as it does now.

Yours truly,
William A. Pintler

```
STATE OF IDAHO    )
                  )
                  ) ss
                  )
COUNTY OF KOOTENAI )
```

Mrs. Katy Dundom-Pintler, being first duly sworn, on her oaths states; "I am the mother of William Augustus Pintler who was born at Wisdom, Beaverhead County, Montana, on July 15, 1885, while my husband Charles E. Pintler and I were passing through Wisdom in a caravan of settlers, the caravan halting during the birth of my son."

Witness my hand this 19th day of May, 1942.

Katie Dundom Pintler

Subscribed and sworn to before me this 19th day of May, 1942, Notary Public in and for the State of Idaho residing at Coeur d' Alene, Idaho. My commission expires July 2, 1945.

H. H. Barton
H. H. Barton
Notary Public for Idaho
Residing at Coeur d'Alene,
My Commission expires June 2, 1945

William Augustus Pintler had to obtain the following affadavits to serve as his birth record   (Shown on pages 141-144)

STATE OF MONTANA)
) ss
COUNTY OF FERGUS)

Mrs. Mary Clark being first duly sworn on oath states;
"I am now a resident of Moore, Montana. On July 15, 1885
I was in Wisdom, Beaverhead County, Montana. On that day
a caravan of settlers was passing through Wisdom. In this
caravan was Charles E. Pintler and Katy Dundom-Pintler, his
wife. The caravan was haulted during which William Augustus
Pintler was born. And I was there."

Witness my hand this 22nd day of May, 1942.

                              Mary Clark

Subscribed and sworn to before me, a duly and authorized and
commissioned Notary Public, for the State of Montana, this
22nd day of May, 1942.

                              L. F. Gimmerby
                        Notary Public in and for the State of
                        Montana.

My commission expires _____ day of _____ 21, 1942

STATE OF IDAHO } SS
COUNTY OF KOOTENAI }

William Augustus Pintler, being first duly sworn, on his oath states, "To the best of my knowledge and belief, I was born in Wisdom, Beaverhead County, Montana on the fifteenth day of July, 1885."

Dated the nineteenth day of June, 1942.

William Augustus Pintler

Subscribed and sworn to before me this 19th day of June, 1942.
Hubert H. Barton
Notary Public for Idaho
My commission expires ___

STATE OF IDAHO } SS
COUNTY OF KOOTENAI }

I, Hubert H. Barton, a duly qualified and commissioned Notary Public in and for the State of Idaho, do hereby certify:

That on this nineteenth day of June, 1942, in corroberation of above affadavit, William Augustus Pintler did exhibit to me four official motor vehicle operators' licenses of the State of Washington, to-wit;

1. Motor vehicle operaters' licenses, 490749, issued to William A. Pintler on April 14, 1930, in which license William A. Pintler gave his age as 44 years.

2. Motor vehicle operators' license, 290379, issued August 82, 1931, to William A. Pintler, in which license he gave his age as forty-six years.

3. Motor vehicle operators' license, 485770, issued to W; A. Pintler on July 12, 1934, in which license he gave his age as forty-eight years.

(Continuation of Notary Public verification of
operator's licenses, submitted by William Augustus
Pintler in corroboration of his affadavit of birth)

4. Motor vehicle operator's license number 332235 issued to William A. Pintler of Newman Lake, Washington on September 2, 1941, in which license the said William A. Pintler gave date of his birth as 1885.

Dated this nineteenth day of June, 1942.

NOTARY PUBLIC IN AND FOR THE STATE OF IDAHO,
RESIDING AT COEUR D'ALENE, IDAHO.
My commission expires June 2, 1945.

ARNOLD OLSEN
1ST DISTRICT, MONTANA

ROOM 1424, LONGWORTH BUILDING
PHONE: 225-3211

COMMITTEES:
POST OFFICE AND CIVIL SERVICE
PUBLIC WORKS

SUBCOMMITTEES:
POSTAL RATES AND
PARCEL POST, CHAIRMAN
CENSUS AND STATISTICS
OPERATIONS
FLOOD CONTROL
ROADS
WATER DEVELOPMENT
SPECIAL SUBCOMMITTEE ON
THE FEDERAL-AID HIGHWAY PROGRAM

Congress of the United States
House of Representatives
Washington, D.C. 20515

February 26, 1969

Mrs. LeRoy Imus
Newman Lake
Washington

Dear Mrs. Imus:

Thank you for your recent letter concerning the proposal that would change the name of the Pintler Wilderness Area to the Robert F. Kennedy Wilderness Area.

I appreciate your taking the time to write to me and express your views. I agree with you that Montana's historical name of the Pintler Wilderness Area should not be changed. I, of course, had the greatest respect for Senator Kennedy, but I think that Montana could honor him another way.

I have asked Senator McKeon to clarify the question you raised. As soon as I receive a reply, I will write to you again.

With kindest personal regards, I am

Sincerely,

Arnold Olsen
ARNOLD OLSEN

AO/tw

UNITED STATES DEPARTMENT OF AGRICULTURE
FOREST SERVICE
Wisdom Ranger District
Wisdom, Montana 59761

2320

January 27, 1978

Mrs. Charlotte McLucas
Rt. #1, Box 26
Newman Lake, WA 99025

Dear Mrs. McLucas:

I was very pleased to receive your letter of January 19, concerning your grandfather Charles E. Pintler.

The map of the Anaconda-Pintlar Wilderness which I have enclosed is dated 1970. It is the latest available map, and is now out of print. There is a very brief reference to your grandfather in the history writeup on the backside of the map. I must confess that that is all I know of Charles Pintler.

If you or your father would send me whatever you know about Charles Pintler I would be most appreciative. As time goes on it becomes much more difficult to correctly document historical fact. Whatever you can document will be made a part of our permanent historical record on the Beaverhead National Forest. This material will then be available for future historians and Forest Service personnel who develop documents such as the Wilderness map.

I have also enclosed a copy of the recently approved Anaconda-Pintlar Wilderness Management Plan. This document will give you an idea about how the Wilderness is being managed, and how it is used by the public.

If you or your father are again in this area please stop by for a visit.

Sincerely,

JOHN J. DOLAN
District Ranger

Enclosures

UNITED STATES DEPARTMENT OF AGRICULTURE
FOREST SERVICE

Wisdom Ranger District
Wisdom, Montana 59761

2320

August 8, 1978

Mrs. Charlotte McLucas
Rt.#1, Box 26
Newman Lake, Washington 99025

Dear Mrs. McLucas;

I'm pleased to say that the Anaconda-Pintler Wilderness is now spelled just that way. The Board of Geographic Names in Washington D.C. has officially recognized the correct spelling. So from now on all reference to Pintler will be correctly spelled.

Thank you for the information that made the change possible.

Sincerely,

JOHN J. DOLAN
District Ranger

Newport Miner 8-31-78

After 41 years they finally got it straight

MISSOULA, Mont. — When the Forest Service created the 158,516-acre Anaconda-Pintlar Primitive Area 41 years ago, Pintlar was misspelled.

Now the U. S. Board of Geographic Names has approved changing the spelling of "Pintlar" to "Pintler."

Evidence was provided by Charles Ellsworth Pintler's granddaughter, Mrs. Paul McLucas of Newman Lake, Wash., confirming that the name of the wilderness and other landmarks in the area should be spelled with an 'e,' the Forest Service said.

The change will be made on signs, maps, and other Forest Service references to the creek, peak, Wilderness, and other geographic points named for the pioneer.

The Wilderness is west of Butte, Mont.

"Pintlar" to "Pintler"

When the Forest Service created the 158,516-acre Anaconda-Pintlar Primitive Area 41 years ago (1937), Pintlar was misspelled.

Wayne H. Valentine, leader of the geometronics group, USDA Forest Service, Northern Region Headquarters, has announced that the U.S. Board of Geographic Names has approved changing the spelling of "Pintlar" to "Pintler."

"Evidence was provided by Charles Ellsworth Pintler's granddaughter, Mrs. Paul McLucas, Newman Lake, Washington, confirming that the name of the Wilderness and other landmarks in the area should be spelled with an 'e.' The Forest Service submitted this evidence to the Board of Geographic Names. The Board has notified us of approval of changing the spelling," Valentine said.

"We are most grateful to Mrs. McLucas for her invaluable assistance," he said. "The changes will be made on signs, maps, and other Forest Service references to the creek, peak, Wilderness, and other geographic points for the pioneer."

The Wilderness is west of Butte, Montana, and extends into the Deerlodge, Beaverhead, and Bitterroot National Forests.

Montana Automobile Association paper (1978)

Anaconda-Pintler Wilderness

An area of 157,803 acres of rugged mountains atop the Continental Divide in Montana noted for its high, barren peaks where mountain goats live.

It is located southwest of Anaconda in the Deerlodge, Beaverhead and Bitterroot National Forests.

Trails lead into it from all sides. Travel the Hiline Trail along the top of the range by foot or horseback. Fish quiet lakes or relax by a mountain brook. Hunt big game with camera or gun.

Information Courtesy U. S. Forest Service

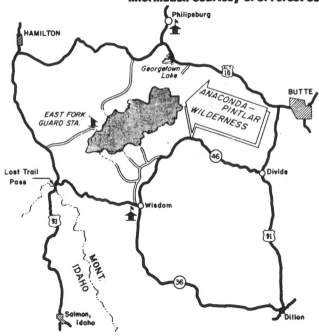

GREAT FALLS (Mont.) TRIBUNE 5-7-78

But it's spelled with an E!

BUTTE (AP) — The Pintlar Scenic Route along U.S. Highway 10A will be dedicated May 21 with Gov. Thomas L. Judge leading a motorcade along the 64-mile stretch from Drummond to Fairmont Hot Springs.

Dean Neitz of Philipsburg, new president of the Scenic Highway 10A Committee, will be master of ceremonies for the day-long event, which includes ribbon cuttings, winings and dinings. The route is said to offer spectacular views of the Continental Divide and Anaconda Pintlar Wilderness areas.

The Anaconda Chamber of Commerce, a principal sponsor, has issued 200 invitations to officials of the Montana Department of Highways and others.

The motorcade will start from Drummond at 10:30 a.m.

Meanwhile, members of the family of Charles Ellsworth Pintler for whom the 159,000-acre wilderness southwest of Anaconda was named are trying to get the U.S. Forest Service to correct its spelling of the family name.

Pintler was born in Winona, Minn., Aug. 30, 1854, and died in Coeur d'Alene, Idaho, in 1925. About 1885, the Pintler family built a cabin in what is now Pintlar Meadows, then moved to Lewistown before going to Idaho in 1915.

Motorcade to Dedicate New Pintler Scenic Route

THE MISSOULIAN April 24, 1978

PHILIPSBURG — A grand-opening motorcade to dedicate the Pintler Scenic Route was announced at a recent meeting of the Philipssburg Chamber of Commerce. Roberta Chandler, Anaconda, a member of the Pinter Scenic Route Committee, said the dedication will take place May 21.

The Scenic Route designation was given to U.S. Highway 10-A between Drummond and Opportunity by the State Highway Commission last fall. Chandler said it is the first such designation in the state.

Ceremonies are scheduled at Drummond, Philipsburg, Gerogetown Lake, Anaconda and the Opportunity interchange on Interstate 90, according to Chandler.

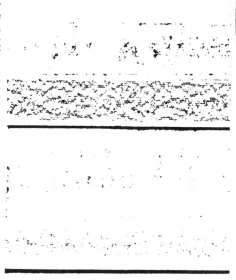

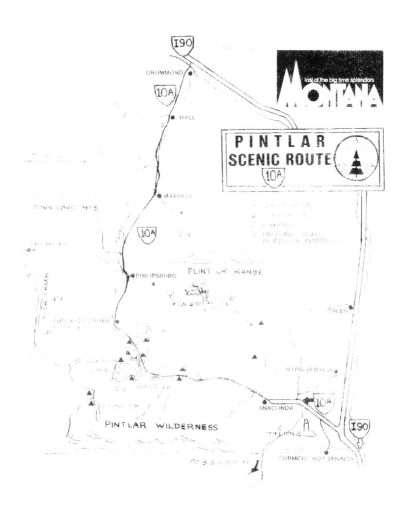

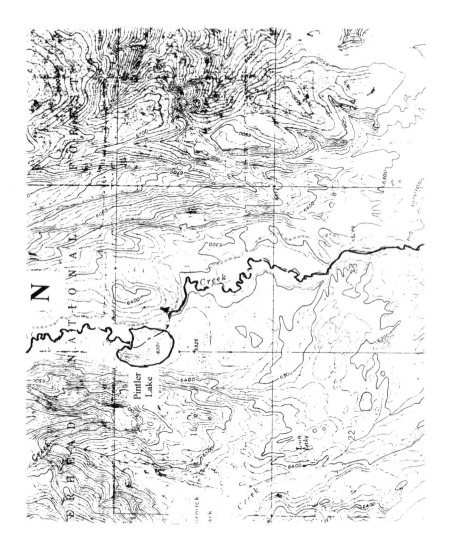

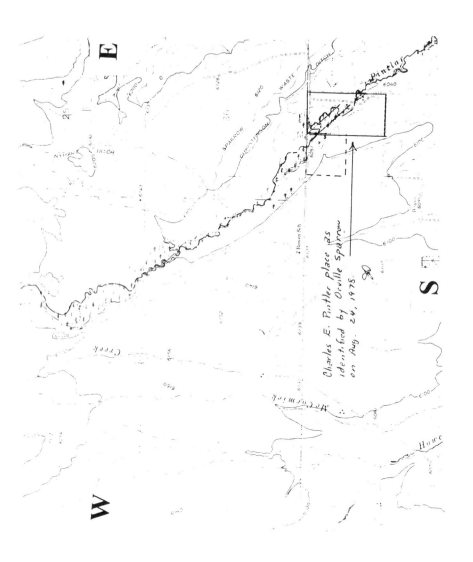

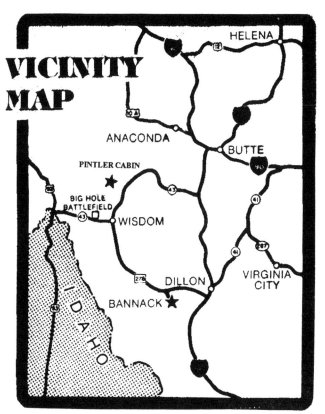

Bannack in relationship with Pintler cabin

Bannack City was famed for the first major gold discovery in 1862. The heyday lasted a short time, but Bannack continued to live on as a frontier mining town. During it's long existance, all manner of humankind have walked through the pages of Bannack's history. Rich in history, today Bannack City is an interesting ghost-town.

Article about Katie's sister, Mary, who attended the trek to Montana Territory in 1885

WEDNESDAY, OCTOBER 21, 1981 — LEWISTOWN NEWS-ARGUS

Lewistown resident may be oldest Montanan

Lewistown is the home of a lady who may possibly be Montana's oldest resident.

She's Mary Clark and she's 107 years old.

Born 14 years before Montana became a state, she has lived almost its entire history since the coming of the white man.

She was born Sept. 16, 1874 near Three Forks, Mont. Her life spans from the days of covered wagon to the days of the modern-day space shuttle.

As a child, her family moved to Washington Territory, near present-day Spokane because they feared Indian attacks in Montana.

They soon discovered, however, that the danger from Indian attacks was just as great in Washington.

At one time, her family was forced to stay at an army stockade for several months for safety purposes.

Mrs. Clark's father then decided to sell his farm to buy 300 horses to sell to settlers arriving to the Montana Territory.

During the five-month journey across the Rocky Mountains, most of the horses died, leaving only a few "tough carcasses" to sell.

Near the end of the journey, her family ran out of food. Reaching Fort Missoula, they received beans, which although hard, "were the best I ever tasted," Mrs. Clark said.

The family settled near Hanover, which was a few miles northeast of Lewistown. Mrs. Clark has continued to make her home in or near Lewistown ever since.

Before moving to the Central Montana Nursing Home, she lived alone. When she well past 90 years old, she still did her own housekeeping, cooking, gardening and milked a cow every day.

Her only daughter died in 1975. She has four grandsons, one granddaughter, Mrs. John Idhe of Lewistown and numerous great grandchildren.

The Story of Pintler Creek

by Bob Weatherly

Part I Continued Next Week

Pintler Creek is one of the branches of George Creek, a main branch of Asotin Creek. George Creek enters Asotin Creek at Jerry, about 3 miles west of Asotin. Pintler Creek joins George Creek about one and one half miles south of Jerry. Pintler Creek heads about 2 miles northwest of Anatone, in the edge of the timbered area and reaches about 10 miles to where it joins George Creek. On the west and on the east the Anatone Flat area with many side gulches joining Pintler. Two of the larger side gulches are Ayers Gulch and Kelly Creek.

At the junction of Pintler Creek and George Creek is the northern end of Myers Ridge, and the foot of the Myers Ridge grade road. Also the location of the... old ranch home of

on a point on the east side of Pintler Creek. Buried there is the infant daughter of George and Myrtle Myers, buried Jan. 13, 1913. Location: in the SE ¼ of the SW ¼ of Sec. 12, Township 9 north, range 45 E. W. M.

It seems that in 1874 Agustus Theodore Pintler, father of Charles and Edwin, settled southeast of Dayton. Records show that he was still there in 1882. In 1878, Charlie and Edwin moved to what was to be Asotin County and each took up adjoining homesteads about 3 miles north and west of Anatone.

Their homesteads were on a nameless creek, in the northern edge of the timbered area of the Blue Mountains. It wasn't long until the creek was known as Pintler Creek. It flowed in a northerly direction, about 10 miles to where it joined with George Creek. The Charlie Pintler homestead was the southwest quarter of Sec. 15, Township 8 north, range 45, E. W.M. A total of 160 acres. Charlie Pintler was born Aug. 30, 1854 in Winona, Minn. In 1870, the family went by covered wagon to Washington Territory. In 1880, Charlie and Katie Cecelia Dundom were married in Lewiston, Idaho.

Edwin Pintler's homestead was: SE ¼ of SW ¼ of Section 10; and the east ½ of the NW ¼, and SW ¼ of NW ¼ of Section 15, Township 8 north, range 45 E. W.M. A total of 160 acres.

What is now known as County Road No. 2480, the Pine Grove Road that goes westerly from Forgey Road, crosses Pintler Creek and by the site of the Pine Grove school, to join the Myers Ridge Road on the west, divided the Pintler property. Edwin's homestead was on the north and Charlies on the south side of this road.

They weren't in the area too long, but long enough to prove up on their homesteads, as each received a patent from the U.S. Land Office.

In July, 1882, Edwin and Mary Pintler sold their place to Fred and Frances Benson for $800.00. In 1903, it was purchased by V.R. Forgey, who transferred it to Robert Forgey in 1941. Records aren't too clear for a few years when it was owned by the Bucholz family, who in turn, sold it to Pearl and Elizabeth Forgey in 1968. They still own it, and Pearl states it is an excellent shaded pasture with good water. There is no sign of the Pintler's buildings, though there "used to be" the remains of a rock fireplace that has disappeared now.

Edwin and Mary Pintler bought some land in northern Garfield County in 1885. It was purchased from James Offield, and was located at the foot of the Beckwith Grade. They had 7 children. Their story would be a chapter in history.

Charlie and Kate Pintler transferred their land in Pintler Creek to one Albert De Lapp, Dec. 7, 1882. He and Kate traded the land for 400 head of horses. He and his father-in-law, Wm. A. Dundon, drove them to Montana.

The Pintler Creek located in Washington Territory

Article on A.T. Pintler found in a supplemental issue of the Dayton Chronicle (February 10, 1888)

A.T. Pintler was officer in Civil War

A.T. Pintler was a native of New York, who had also made his home in Michigan and Minnesota, before pioneering in Columbia County with his wife, Eliza Phoebe Pomeroy Pintler.

Mr. Pintler was born in 1830; his wife in 1837. They were wed in Minnesota.

The years that followed, according to Mrs. Pintler's obituary, were difficult. Mr. Pintler enlisted in the Civil war in 1861, and earned the rank of lieutenant before his discharge.

In his absence, Mrs. Pintler was left in charge of the couple's farm, which was in sparsely settled country. During this time, she withstood Indian attacks, which scattered most of her neighbors.

In the later part of 1863, according to her obituary, she learned that her husband was injured, and laid up near Vicksburg. "She immediately left for the front and finding him in very critical condition, she nursed him for three months, when, in 1864 he resigned his commission...and returned with her to their home."

They departed for the Northwest in 1872, spending the winter of 1874 in the Rocky Mountains. The arrived in Columbia County in the mid-1870's, and settled on a farm near Balleysburg.

The Pintlers had eight children, but two died in infancy. Two remained in Columbia County, including Nellie Pintler, who married another pioneer—Jacob Rainwater.

Mrs. Pintler died August 27, 1891. In 1893 Mr. Pintler left Columbia County and eventually remarried. He died in Elk City, Oregon on October 25, 1911 at the age of 81.

Inscription on tombstone of Eliza Pomeroy Pintler—Dayton, Territory of Washington

We miss thee from our home, dear Mother
We miss thy tender care
Our home is dark without thee Mother
We miss thee everywhere

Articles pertaining to parents of Charles Ellsworth Pintler

GONE EAST.—Thursday evening, A. J. Dexter and A. T. Pintler, started for a weeks' visit to the land beyond the Rockies. They will go direct to Pennsylvania. Mr. Pintler will first visit his sister at Easton, Wayne county, whom he has not seen since July 1849, over thirty-seven years ago. He will then call on another sister at Cold Water, Michigan, and will see a part of Wisconsin before his return. Mr. Dexter will first stop at ___ry, in the oil regions, and then come ___ck to Iowa. Mrs. Dexter's mother will ___ company him on his return home. The CHRONICLE's best wishes go with these ___ veterans on their long journey to re-___it the scenes of long ago.

157

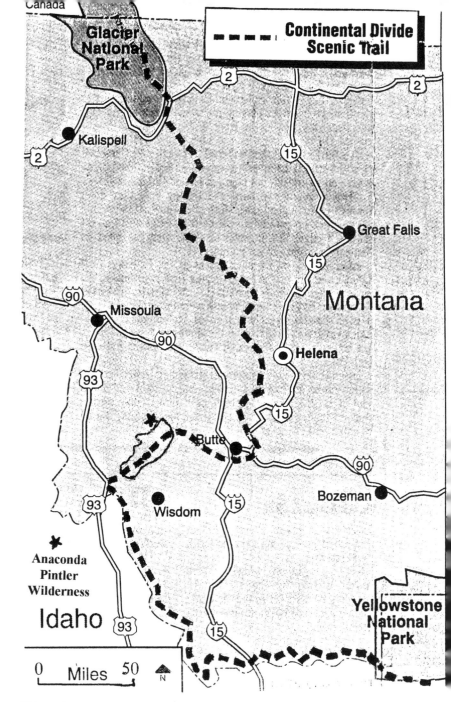

This trail will eventually link Canada and Mexico (Spokesman Review-1997)

BIBLIOGRAPHY AND RESOURCES

Books
Beecher, Edmund T., *Spokane Corona Eras and Empires*, C. W. Hill, 1974.
Berthold, Mary Paddock., *Big Hole Journal*, Harlo Press, Detroit, Michigan, 1974.
Berthold, Mary Paddock., *Turn Here For The Big Hole*, Harlow Press, Detroit, Michigan, 1974.
El Hult, Ruby., *Steamboats In The Timber*, Binsford and Mort, Portland, Oregon, 1952.
Evans, C. B., *Another Montana Pioneer*, Bickley Printing Co., Pasadena, California, 1960.
Evans, C. B., *Western Pioneer Home Life*, Economy Printing Concern, Inc., Berne, Indiana, 1965.
Forbis, William H., *The Cowboys, Time Life Books*, The Old West, Alexandria, Virginia, 1973.
Gilbert, Bil., *The Trailblazers*, Time Life Books, The Old West, Alexandria, Virginia, 1973.
Hamilton, James McClellan, History of Montana, *From Wilderness To Statehood*, Binsford and Mort, Portland, Oregon, 1952.
Hauck, Betty, *Gold On A Shoestring*, Montana, 1982.
Howard, Josseph Kinsey, *Montana, High Wide And Handsome*, Yale University Press, New Haven, Connecticutt, 1959.
Horn, Huston, *The Pioneers*, Time Life Books, The Old West, Canada, 1974.
Lang, William L., Malone, Michael P., Roeder, Richard, *A History of Two Centuries*, University of Washington Press, Seattle and London, 1991.
Montana State University, *The Montana Almanac*, State University Press, Misssoula, Montana, 1957.
Schantes, Carol A., *In The Mountain Shadows*, University of Nebraska Press, Lincoln, Nebraska, 1991.

Tanner, Ogden, *The Ranchers*, The Old West, Time Life Books, Canada, 1974.

Toole, Ross K. *Montana, An Uncommon Land*, University of Oklahoma Press, Norman, Oklahoma, 1959.

Vankson, Russel A., and Harrison, Lester S., *Beneath These Mountains*, Vantage Press, New York, Washington, Hollywood, 1966.

Walker, Bryce S. *The Great Divide, The American Wilderness*, Time Life Books, Alexandaria, Virginia, 1973.

Brochures
United States Department of Interior, "Soldiers and Brave", Washington, D.C., National Parks Service, 1971.

United States Department of Agriculture, "Search for Solitude", Our Wilderness Heritage, United States Printing Office, Washington, D.C., June, 1970.

United States Department of Agriculture Forest Service, "The Anaconda-Pintlar Wilderness Management Plan", 1977-1987, Beaverhead, Bitterroot and Deerlodge National Forests Northern Regions.

Other Resources, Maps and Plats, Correspondence, Newspaper Clippings, Interviews, and Unpublished Papers
Beckes, Michael R., United States Department of Agriculture Forest Service, Regional Archaeologist Forest Service, Missoula, Montana.

Bergstrom, Dennis, Reference Department, Spokane Valley Library, Spokane, Washington.

Carlson, John F., Garfield County Courthouse, Pomeroy, Washington.

Carson, Liz, Genealogist and Historian, Dayton Memorial Library, Dayton, Washington.

Columbia County Courthouse, Dayton, Wahington.

Dolan, John J., United States Department of Agriculture Forest Service, District Ranger, Wisdom, Montana.

Egger, Bruce E., United States Department of Agriculture Forest Service, District Ranger, Pomeroy Ranger District, Pomeroy, Washington.

Hanson, Valerie J., Clerk and Recorder, Beaverhead County Courthouse, Dillon, Montana.

Havig, Dennis K., United States Department of Agriculture Forest Service, Wisdom, Ranger District, Wisdom, Montana.

Karr, Raymond W., United States Department of Agriculture Forest Service, Director-Information Office, Federal Building, Missoula, Montana.

Keyes, Duane, Wisdom, Montana.

Kittredge, William, University of Montana, Missoula, Montana.

Kootenai County Court House, Coeurd'Alene, Idaho.

Moore, Judson, United Department of Agriculture Forest Service, Regional Headquarters, Missoula, Montana.

Nez Perce County Court House, Lewiston, Idaho.

Quiring, Mary Ann, Historian, Lewistown, Montana.

Rathbun, May, County Clerk and Records, Fergus County Court House, Lewistown, Montana.

Ryan, J. Michael, United States Department of Agriculture Forest Service, Forest Archaeologist, Beaverhead and Deerlodge National Forests Dillon, Montana.

Shovers, Brian, Reference Historian, Montana Historical Society Library, Helena, Montana.

Smith, LaDoris, Asotin County Courthouse, Asotin, Washington.

Smith, Lynn, Asotin County Court House, Asotin, Washington.

Spritzer, Don, Reference Department, Missoula Library, Missoula, Montana.

United States Department of Agriculture Forest Service, AWilderness, Recreation and Heritage Resources, Missoula, Montana.

United States Board of Geographic Names, Washington, D.C. and Reston, Virginia.

Weatherly, Robert P., Historian, Director of the Asotin County Historical Society, Asotin, Washington.

Personal thanks for the information the following persons contributed
Sally Campbell, Helena, Montana, for her helpful advice.

Jack Gilluly, Anaconda, Montana, for sharing reference material and corresondence.

John Ihde and Edna Kizer, "Bits and Pieces," Dundom Family History, Lewistown, Montana.

Dorothy Kent, Lewistown, Montana, for her worthwhile correspondence and news articles.

Floyd N. McCallum, Rathdrum, Idaho, for sharing regional history and memories.

Richard W. Pintler, Monument, Colorado, for sharing genealogy records and contributing his part in the Senate resolution against changing the name of the wilderness to another.

We have endeavored to include any person that contributed information in the writing of this book and if we overlooked anyone, we apologize.

Additional copies are $12.95 plus $3.00 shipping and handling.

Make check or money order payable to:

The Gilted Edge
P.O. Box 484
Newman Lake, WA 99025-0484